START *Living* AGAIN

Saranya Umakanthan

FiNGERPRINT!

Published by
FiNGERPRINT!
An imprint of Prakash Books India Pvt. Ltd

113/A, Darya Ganj,
New Delhi-110 002
Email: info@prakashbooks.com/sales@prakashbooks.com

[f] Fingerprint Publishing
[X] @FingerprintP
[O] @fingerprintpublishingbooks
www.fingerprintpublishing.com

ISBN: 978 93 5856 675 8

To Lord Shiva

The powerhouse of energy,
The symbol of permanency,
The lightness and the darkness,
The divine love,
The world,
The universe,
The one who has shown me that
miracles are indeed possible;
The one who will stay with me forever and
beyond;
I owe everything I hold precious to you;
And that includes my writing;
I love you, Shiva. Om Namah Shivayah!
Har Har Mahadev!

Prologue

"We are not meant to be . . ." Anshik Dhawan's heart pained to say those words, yet he did.

The evening sun was gradually sinking into the sky. Darkness took over and enveloped them. The chirping of the birds had died down. Apart from the crushed leaves underneath them, the ambiance was strangely silent inside the Broken Trishul temple. A feeling of loneliness strangled him even before he could break up. Though they had never named their relationship for years, he had admired its beauty and derived strength from it. He concealed his sorrow with a calm exterior, but his regret was evident in his eyes. His soul ached, making it difficult for him to breathe.

Apt for what they were going through, Ananya wore her knee-length black dress. She lost her smile at his words. Holding him by his

T-shirt collar, she asked, "Is this the end? Do you want me to leave?"

He wanted to deny her statement loud and clear, but he did not. How could he? The promise he had made to his mother loomed in front of him, daring him to break it.

Despite his internal struggle, he pushed her away. She tightly clasped his hands for one last time, seemingly unwilling to let him go. Tears welled up in her eyes and then dripped onto his hands.

Anshik experienced a complete breakdown. Melancholy swept over him as he turned to face the opposite side, his shoulders sagging. In desperation, he covered his forehead with his hands.

She spoke from behind, "Look into my eyes and tell me that what we shared was not love."

He wanted to shout that it was beyond love. Their hearts were forever intertwined in that relationship. Yet he did not.

The pain intensified, and he rolled restlessly on the king-size bed. Finally surrendering to his feelings, he pleaded desperately, "Ananya, please don't leave me . . . I need you."

Her beautiful face vanished, and he got up from his bed, sweating. This dream kept killing him for three long years. Hearing the voice of her son, Sheela Dhawan ran to his room.

"Anshik, are you alright?"

Silence.

"The same dream?"

She deciphered her answer by looking into his eyes.

"Sorry, *beta* . I shouldn't have interfered and played God; I thought I was leading you in the right direction but ended up messing your life."

He did not want to listen to this confession.

Comprehending her son's anger, she said, "Anshik . . . I don't want to hold you to my promise anymore."

He opened his eyes wide in bewilderment.

"*Beta*, you have attained the exact position you aspired for. It is time to step into the next phase of your life now. Go on; no one is stopping you. Definitely not me. I made a mistake once and do not want to make another."

His mother's words pulled him out of his reverie. She caught hold of his hands, lending her support. Turning toward her, he hugged and buried his face in her shoulders.

Sheela believed her strong-willed son was emotionally damaged and blamed herself for his predicament. Her touch was gentle as she ruffled his hair and patted his back.

"It was difficult, ma."

"To let her go?"

He gave her a slight nod.

"Do you still love her?"

"I never stopped."

"Are you angry with me, *beta*?"

He thought about it. "No. You did what you felt was right. Sometimes circumstances overrule us."

"What's keeping you tied to the past, then? The reasons that held you back don't exist anymore." She was right. His eyes flickered with a tiny flame of hope.

"At twenty-seven, you are not the same Anshik Dhawan you were three years ago. I am proud of my responsible son, who sacrificed whatever he held dear and took care of this family. But now it is time, Ansh, for you to bring back what you lost," prompted Sheela.

"But what if I am too late?"

"Don't worry. God never gives up on people who trust him."

Processing the positivity in her statement, he smiled as his eyes crinkled in the corners.

"Hah, finally, I see the smile I love. Get ready. Your dad is all set to attend the inauguration ceremony of your new office. Being the boss, you can't afford to be late."

CHAPTER 1

The End

When everything goes downhill, and you tumble into the sea of depression; just hold on to the rope of hope and climb back to life.

Dressed royally in a collared *kurti*, Ananya confidently walked around the set. Known as the 'TV queen,' her show garnered popularity among Indian viewers. She was overjoyed that the viewers were embarking on an emotional journey alongside the couple—Vivian and Samaira, the protagonists of her television series. They joined in laughter with them and sympathized by shedding tears when challenges arose in their lives. Witnessing Viv and Sam in a tender moment on the screen made her completely forget herself. Ananya released a contented sigh. This was what she wanted in her life—to bring beautiful stories onto the screens of viewers, channel their emotions, and steer them in the right direction. The influence of her story had made her a household name, and she noticed a Bollywood star waiting to meet her. "Cut."

They wound up the show's last scene for the day. "Ma'am, today's sequence has turned out perfectly," her assistant congratulated her. Accepting his wishes gracefully, Ananya stretched her arms, and her fingers hit the nearby glass vase on the corner table.

"Ouch." Her voice was half-muffled, and she woke up to see her bleeding fingers. The soul-stirring dream vanished directly from her line of sight. The wound didn't hurt, but she felt down because her instincts told her something terrible was on the horizon.

She tried her hardest to push the disturbing thought out of her mind.

"Gosh, it felt real." Her soul seemed stuck in her dream.

"Enough, Ananya. Get going! Today is going to be the best day of your life. Who knows what might happen?"

With the self-inspiring instruction giving way to a rush of bountiful energy inside her, she got up from her bed to attend to her cut. She was eagerly looking forward to this day. Moving from Shivapur to Pune, she was a village girl at heart. The beautiful and pleasant city had transformed her and strengthened her dreams, yet she stayed simple. Into her final year of digital filmmaking course, which she was pursuing against her parents' wishes, she had a chance to reach her goals with today's event. The college placement cell had invited Aditya, a 55-year-old movie director with a string of successful Bollywood films the previous year. Rumor had it that he wanted to venture into the TV industry and needed a remarkable script. The placement cell had lured him to their campus, tempting him to headhunt for fresh and creative minds. The students had their scripts ready. This could be a make-or-break for anyone in their class. Ananya's choice was the one she had considered her best so far. She had worked on her script for the past six months and knew it was jam-packed with emotions that could entice viewers. Some students were about to present their scripts individually, but she was about to do hers with Kishore—her scripting partner, though he wanted to be more than that. Thinking about him brought a smile onto her face.

Kishore was a fun-loving person who would do anything for her, or at least that's what she believed. She did not know if he was serious when he half-heartedly professed his love. Together, they wrote multiple scripts for their college cultural competitions. Ananya created the story, and Kishore added a layer of humor surrounding the events. Though the script they would present today did not require a comedy track, Kishore had requested that she check if such an addition was possible. Despite her refusal of his love for now, Ananya had a soft spot for him, and when he requested to include him in the presentation, she handed over the script yesterday without a second thought. Today, their lives might change altogether. And who knows? Someday, she might collaborate with him professionally and end up together on a personal note. Not wanting to explore further, she ran to board a shared auto to get to her college.

Time: 10 a.m., Entertainment Hall, College of Digital Filmmaking, Pune.

The director had already shown up. Wearing a collared blue cotton kurti as in her dream, she completed her look with matching earrings and cut-out black heels. At five feet five, she was tall, and her fair skin was flushed with excitement. Her round face added volume to her glowing cheeks, which enhanced her attractiveness. With her hair loose, she entered the room where the students were deeply conversing about their scripts with Mr. Aditya, who was dressed in a casual white shirt and black pants. She had confirmed to Kishore that she would be in by ten, and they could present their script together.

She greeted Kishore with a wave, noticing that he was in the other corner. But to her surprise, he neither acknowledged her presence nor waved back, and she was pretty sure that he had seen her, seated five feet away. Her friend, Riya, interrupted her.

"Hey, Ananya. You are late. Mr. Aditya came in sharply by nine."

"Nine? Did he come early? He was supposed to come by ten." Ananya frowned.

"Who said so? Didn't you check the notice board yesterday?"

"But Kishore told me the director would come only by ten," Ananya told Riya.

"Oh, but Kishore came early and has already discussed his script with Mr. Aditya. In fact, he was the first one to do it."

Ananya gasped. This could not happen to her. Seeing her worried face, Riya inquired, "What happened?"

"That . . . that was *my* script, Riya!" Tears engulfed her eyes.

"It might not be. He might have presented his own," countered Riya as a gruff voice interrupted them.

"Students, I have heard multiple stories from you all so far, but I have already given my heart to the first script that I heard today from Kishore, and I don't want to waste the time of others," he made his intention clear.

Though disappointed, the students cheered for Kishore, exhibiting fair play.

"Wow, Kishore. What is the name of the winning script?" Riya asked for confirmation.

Pushing his glasses closer to his eyes, Aditya ruffled through the papers and read the script's title, "The Gift of Treachery by Kishore Karwal."

Riya turned to Ananya and observed her disappointment.

"Don't worry," she consoled, looking at her distressed state.

Ananya lifted her head. With her shoulders held high, she wiped away her tears and walked directly toward Kishore, who had a triumphant, sneaky smile.

"Congratulations!" she wished.

"Thanks." There was not an ounce of regret on his face.

Opportunities in her field were rare, and she had lost the golden goose of her career. All just because she had trusted the wrong person. Desperation welled up within her. How could someone who professed to love her backstab her? Her panicked thoughts made her reminisce about her father's words.

'One day, you will regret that you threw away the life I had set up for you and chose to make an earning out of your stories, which you could never do. Is this even a dream, for God's sake? Are you living in one of your stories? A girl must be a respectful wife in a decent family. Mark my words once and for all—you will come back running to me once you realize that chasing your stupid dreams in a city is not that easy and is not required for a girl. That is when I will slam my door at you for insulting me by not being a dutiful daughter.'

The words elicited a pain that she tried her best to suppress. Will her father's curse come true? No one would believe it if she told others that the script was hers. They would conclude that it was her jealousy talking. She stepped into her hostel with a regretful sigh.

The hostel she had stayed at was near her college and the teashop, where she worked in the evening to take care of her expenses in the city and to pay her fees. Her room was on the ground floor, and she shared it with Maitri, who was struggling to find a job after completing her engineering degree.

The warden called her from the reception. She was a lady in her late forties with curly hair tied together into a bun and wore a red cotton sari. The big red *bindi* on her forehead terrified the girls at the hostel.

"Good that you are back, Ananya. I was waiting for you."

"Ma'am, the money is ready."

"Thank goodness. At least you remember that you must pay the hostel fee for the past three months," she scorned.

Controlling her anger against the warden's sarcasm, she provided her reason. "Ma'am, the teashop owner I work for needed money for a lung operation. Hence, he could not pay me."

"*Oho*, stop your sob story. Should I suffer because he got operated on?" She twisted her lips in anger.

"No, ma'am, I didn't mean it that way. But don't worry. I have your fees ready. He gave it to me yesterday."

The warden smiled. "Bring it to me. Don't make me wait. After paying, clean your room. Your roommate, Maitri, vacated the room this morning. "

Why did Maitri vacate without telling her? What was the necessity? She had to call and check if she was alright. But before that, she had to pay her fees. If not, the warden would not mind throwing her out. All that mattered to her was money, and she did not blame her for that; after all, it was her business.

She entered her room and frowned as her bag was on top of the rack instead of the bottom shelf, where she had placed it before leaving. Probably, Maitri had cleaned the room before leaving. She dipped her hands inside to retrieve her purse. She did not find any.

Twitching her eyebrows, she searched again, but in vain.

"Where did the purse go?" She remembered keeping her hard-earned money, which she had received from Amar *bhaiya,* safely inside the purse. She needed those fifteen thousand rupees to pay her hostel fees. Her forehead sweated despite Pune's pleasant climate. Tension twisted her nerves into knots. Her mind recalled a snippet of Maitri's phone conversation with her boyfriend yesterday.

'I promise that I'll arrange the money for you somehow, darling . . .'
'Fifteen thousand? That would not be a problem.'

The words that had sounded lovey-dovey yesterday now threatened her. She connected the dots and figured out why Maitri had fled without letting her know. The day was turning into a nightmare. Maitri was gone, and so was her money.

The warden got impatient waiting for her and came to her room. "My dear *Maharani,* how much time should I wait? Where is the money?"

"Did Maitri leave any contact details?" she queried, looking for the only way out.

"Have you gone mad? How does it even answer my query? She did not give me any contact details, and as she had already settled her fees, I did not ask her. Now, where is the money, Ananya?"

"Ma'am, I don't have the money. Someone has stolen it."

"Stolen by whom?" the warden screamed at the top of her voice.

"Maitri ."

"Do you have any proof?"

"No, ma'am but if you can give me some time—" she pleaded.

The warden raised her hands to stop her tirade.

"I am sick of hearing your excuses, Ananya. Enough! Stop throwing the blame at someone else."

Angrily, the warden took her bag and dragged her out of the room. She opened the bag and took out the file containing her educational certificates. Her voice had brought several girls out of their rooms, watching her with sympathy.

She threw the bag with a thud. "Ananya, I did not believe you could stoop this low, blaming Maitri for your misdemeanor. What did you do with the money? Spent it partying with your boyfriend? I know how the girls of this generation behave," she condemned.

"But, ma'am . . . ," Ananya's voice wobbled with embarrassment.

"Don't come back without bringing the pending fees. Till then, your certificates will be safe with me."

She shoved Ananya out through the entrance. Her script and money were stolen by two people she had considered friends. With no money or place to live, Ananya walked out in tears. Her dreams shattered before her very eyes.

"Why is life unfair toward me? What harm did I ever do to anyone?" There were no reasonable answers to the questions born out of her desperation.

CHAPTER 2

The Black Day

When trouble doubles or triples, remember that even tripled trouble does not stay forever in this temporary world.

Ananya forced herself to calm down. She was unable to think rationally. She needed money to get back to her hostel and retrieve her certificates. Hardly a week was left in the last semester, and she had to complete her degree. Her brain processed her next move. Quickly, an idea hit her. She could ask Amar *bhaiya* for an advance on her salary. She ran to the teashop where she worked.

The sight of the teashop took Ananya aback. Surrounded by officials and a bulldozer nearby, she could see it was partly demolished. She was stunned to see Amar *bhaiya* in tears.

"Stop them, please. This is my livelihood," the old man pleaded with folded hands. At sixty, he had no other alternative. With all the hassle, his work clothes were filthy and tattered. "*Bhaiya*, what happened?" Ananya ran to him.

"They are destroying my shop, Ananya!"

"But why?"

An official said, "You think you made a smart move when you put up your shop in front of this corporate building? It's an encroached property, and we have received a complaint from them."

Amar shivered despite wearing an old cardigan.

"The employees prefer tea from your shop rather than the ones inside. That might be another reason they've raised this complaint," the officials told them sympathetically, yet they did their duty.

Ananya held Amar's shivering hands.

"Is she somehow involved in this encroachment?" the official asked Amar.

"No, no . . . let her go," he told them desperately.

"But—"

Amar halted Ananya with his words. "Leave. Don't get your future entangled with all this legal drama."

"*Bhaiya*—"

"I said leave," he commanded.

With all her hopes dashed again, she left the shop. Feeling sympathetic for the old man, she walked further into the busy streets. That is when she realized that not only had Amar lost his livelihood, but so had she, as it was her only source of income. The day's blackness increased by a notch.

She considered asking Riya for money, but how would she repay her if she had no means of earning it? She held her forehead nervously. An auto honked as she struggled to move aside to the corner.

Dejection weighed her down. She looked up. It was dark, and clouds loomed over her. What made a bright day suddenly become so dark? The only option that was left was to ask her mother. She was her sole support, although her father had reprimanded and cursed her for her career choice. Her village, Shivapur, was just 40 minutes away. She had a few currency notes in her college bag in case of an emergency. And she was undoubtedly in that situation. She rushed to catch a bus.

Ananya's hands trembled as she rapped on the door, silently pleading for her mother to open it.

"Ananya?" her mother queried in surprise when she saw her.

Mrs. Pooja Mehta cast a glance back and saw her husband in the garden. She hurriedly closed the main door and slightly pushed her daughter out.

"Happy to see you, dear. Are you okay? What do you want? Be quick before your father sees you."

"Is he still angry at me?"

"You know about him. He wants you to fail and come back."

"But, ma, is it wrong for me to dream, being a girl?"

"We don't have time for this discussion, Ananya."

"I need some money to pay my hostel fees. My roommate stole it from me," she stated in a whisper.

Without further queries, Mrs. Pooja Mehta understood her daughter's predicament. She quickly came out with a stash of cash.

"Ma, thank you," she cried.

The door opened again with a thud.

"What are you doing here?" Mr. Mehta's stern voice broke their tender moment, and Ananya jumped in guilt.

Snatching the money back from her hands, he turned to his wife. "How dare you?" Mr. Mehta slapped her hard.

Pooja held her hand over her cheek and responded, "You don't understand. She needs—"

"I don't care what she needs. She knows what she needs, and that does not include us or our money."

Ananya stopped his tirade. "Yes, I know what I need, papa, but never raise your hand again on ma. I will not tolerate that."

Turning to her mother, she said, "It is okay, ma. I'll manage in some way. You take care."

Ananya came back to the city with a heavy heart. It was four in the evening. Her mind forgot to remind her that she had not had a single morsel of food the entire day.

Kishore stole her script and snatched the only opportunity in sight. Maitri's theft left her without money, causing the warden to kick her out of the hostel and leave her homeless. Her certificates were seized. With Amar *bhaiya's* teashop demolished, her source of income was destroyed. On top of it, she tasted her father's wrath today. Each second became intolerable.

Her strength slowly ebbed out of her, and she walked soullessly on the main road, ignoring the honking vehicles. Tears drenched her swollen face. All the paths on her road appeared to be blocked. She hit her hand in frustration and wanted to tell someone about her problems.

'Let me call Riya,' she thought.

As she fumbled to take out her mobile from her bag, she failed to notice the speeding auto behind, which appeared out of nowhere. Otherwise, the road was deserted.

"*Arre*, move!" the auto driver shrieked and honked.

The side of the auto hit her at full throttle, causing her to fall against the electric post. Her bag and mobile were thrown away. She writhed to get up, but the driver did not stop.

"Sorry, lady. Need to rush." She heard his voice as the auto sped away.

Her forehead hurt, and it took her a moment to grasp that she had been involved in an accident. Her fingers gently probed her head and sensed the wetness of her blood. Somehow, this appeared insignificant compared to the troubles she had gone through earlier in the day.

She struggled to get up and faltered. Holding onto the post, she gave it one more try. A couple of men ran toward her. She believed they were coming to help, so she extended her hands.

They ducked underneath and picked up her bag and mobile.

"Hey," she screamed.

But it fell on deaf ears. Her belongings were gone, including her mobile.

'What kind of world are we living in?'

Her mind criticized as she fought to stand straight against the post. Knowing it was futile to chase them, she continued her aimless walk with absolutely nothing.

Along with the things she lost today, she had also lost her hope and trust. She had no more tears to shed, and she felt empty.

'What is the point of this struggle?' she thought weakly.

Her tired legs took her somewhere, and she sat on the side of the road. A coin hit her squarely in the face. She looked up, dazed, to see that she was sitting next to a group of beggars.

"Are you okay?" one of them asked in a kind voice. She looked at her state. With her torn dress and bleeding forehead, she could not blame them for taking her as one.

From dreaming of being a TV queen in her dreams to sitting with the beggars in reality, she had tumbled down a long way in a day. Regret overwhelmed her.

Her mind had brought her unconsciously to this place. The temple of Broken Trishul was nearby. Furiously, she limped to the temple, where she had met her so-called friend many times and shared her love and dreams.

With folded hands in front of God, she screamed, "What did I do? Did I hurt someone? If not, why are these dreadful events happening in my life? Or is this because of the sins I have committed in my past life? Is it the doing of bad karma?"

Wiping away her tears furiously, she continued, "Gosh! I don't understand my destiny. Is it a sin that I was born a girl? Was it wrong of me to expect support from my dear ones? Oh, God, are you even hearing me?"

Thumping the iron rod close by, she whispered in pain, "Be happy that you have broken me! I am tired of fighting and sick of my repetitive failures. What is the purpose of living when I've nothing to look forward to?"

She had lost her courage, the essential trigger toward a better life. With soulless eyes, she begged, "*Shivji*, why don't you bless me with death?" She broke down, sobbing uncontrollably.

*****

The Broken Trishul temple was only known to a few. The public could not easily see the abandoned old stone temple since dense trees hid it. It was named after the Shiva idol inside, which had a broken brass *trishul*. Only people who lived nearby knew that such a temple existed. Anshik Dhawan was one of them. This was where his dreams began, and he was living his dream today. His company, TechWarriors, had opened yet another branch in Pune to meet the client demands, and he was overjoyed at the expanding client base. Having started from the ground up, the company now employs nearly 3,000 people. He had come here to perform a small pooja for *Shivji* and to thank him for this new opportunity.

But he had paid an enormous price for this success. He had lost Ananya in pursuit of his dreams, the only soul who stood by him when he had absolutely nothing. Thinking of her made his heart flutter.

Was she married now? He frowned. He could not imagine her with anyone else, but the circumstances had pushed him to let her go. However, she had made an unerasable mark on him. She was the one who had told him that he was born to rule this world.

"Promise me. Start living again." She had nudged him to do so at this same place three years ago when he was about to give up. They had sealed their promise with a kiss, which spoke of gratitude, love, and desire.

"*Shivji*, please give me another chance . . . bring her back into my life." He prayed sincerely, not realizing it would be answered with lightning speed.

Anshik could not believe his eyes as he walked in. Standing with her back toward him was Ananya. With her dress torn at her shoulders and her drooped stance, he was not initially sure. Most of all, he could not believe that the girl who had such energetic vibes was wishing for her death. But her voice confirmed her identity.

'*God, this is not the girl I knew.*'

"Ananya." She froze on hearing his voice. She turned slowly to look at him after three long years. He observed her pale, tear-drenched face and bleeding forehead.

"Anshik!" she gasped.

He was the last person she had expected to see. Today's happenings took a toll on her, and she felt giddy. She tried her best to steady herself. But her hunger and misery pulled the plug on her. The world around her darkened, and she fell to the ground with a thud.

"Ananya . . . Anu, are you okay?" He reacted instantly and rushed to her.

CHAPTER 3

A Way Out

*Even amidst difficult circumstances, dance if you
ever get a chance to bring back your stance.*

He had always dreamed of holding Ananya again, but not in these circumstances. With her faint body in his arms, he shivered despite his muscular frame. Leaving her at the same spot for a few seconds, he hurried to his car. Coming back with a can of water and a towel, he splashed water on her face.

"Ananya," he called, tapping her face gently.

That brought her back to her senses as she struggled to open her eyelids.

"Are you alright?" he asked as she sat on the stone floor of the temple. With her hands on her forehead, the unfortunate events of her day overwhelmed her thoughts.

"What are you doing here, Anshik?"

Squatting beside her with his knees up, he lifted her face with his long, lean fingers. "I am asking you the same, Ananya. What happened to you?"

"Nothing."

"Don't talk rubbish. What went wrong?" His anxiety was visible in his eyes.

"Everything. Fate snatched my life just like that with no pity. But why should I even tell you? Who are you to me?"

"How dare you ask me that?" his voice increased by a notch.

Ananya realized he was asking about her torn dress, the dirt traces on her body, and the wound. Weakness gripped her, yet she turned to him.

Over six feet tall, he appeared taller than the last time she had seen him. With a lean, rugged face and a sharp nose, Anshik was handsome. His branded blazer and Rolex watch screamed that he had amassed wealth. His olive-skinned complexion and broad eyebrows gave him a brooding look that exhibited his manliness.

"Why does it even matter to you?"

He shook his face in anger. "Don't bring out our old squabble now."

"Is that what you term it?"

"I hate arguments. Look at you, for God's sake. Come on, get up." With those words, he caught hold of her shoulders and helped her to stand up. Accepting his support grudgingly, she limped to the stone bench under the trees.

After taking their seats next to each other, a strange silence enveloped them. But there was a time when they had sat in the same bench and laughed wholeheartedly. Ananya's heart trembled at the thought of being overwhelmed by memories. He took a bar of chocolate from his pocket.

"This chocolate was given to me for the opening of my second branch office in Pune. Have a bite. It appears as if you have not eaten for days."

"I don't want your sympathy, Mr. Anshik Dhawan."

"And you are not getting it, Miss Ananya Mehta. It's still Miss, right?"

As he awaited her response, his heart pounded painfully. Even with her hair out of place and dirt smeared on her face, her innocence projected her innate beauty.

He noted that she did not wear a *mangalsutra*. He heaved a relieved sigh. But what if she was in a relationship with someone? His hands tightened at that disturbing thought.

"Tell me, Ananya," he prompted.

"Why are you asking me queries like you are my elder brother?"

"I never was, and I never want to be."

Her heart skipped a beat with his declaration. But anger dominated and took over.

"Hah, I remember now. You are my friend. That is what you labeled our relationship earlier," she criticized.

"I am still your friend. You were the one who completely cut off my contact."

His eyes blazed with rage. Ten minutes with her, she was activating all his hormones, including his temper.

"I don't allow my friends to intrude into my private life."

She snatched the chocolate from his hands. "Do you even know what I went through today? Or are you showing off that you have done well for yourself?"

Guessing her intentions, Anshik took the chocolate back before she could throw it. "No, you are not throwing food; you are the same headstrong Ananya underneath. That is why I am surprised to see you broken."

Bringing his fingers close to her lips, he forced her to have a couple of pieces of the chocolate despite her reluctance.

Ananya sighed. What was the point of arguing with him over a piece of chocolate?

He noted that the fiery spirit in her eyes was gone, and it had turned soulless as her resistance waned. This was not the time to point that out. He dipped a tiny towel into the water. For a powerful man, he wiped her face tenderly with the towel and removed the streaks of blood and dirt. "Please tell me, Anu."

His tender words undid her. Droplets of tears engulfed her eyes. He wiped them away, unaware that he was doing so. He was devastated by her sadness. It was as if they had never been apart these three years.

"Don't cry," he whispered. Hiding her pain, she turned to the other side.

"Anshik, I tried my best, yet I failed. I fought back against all odds, but nothing worked out. In short, I have nothing— neither money nor a career. My parents have given up on me, and what I believed to be love was a sham. I don't have a roof over my head. And the worst part of it all, or the best part, is that everything happened in a day!"

Slowly, she walked him over on what she had gone through that horrifying day. She had his complete attention as she opened up.

"Is it wrong to trust people?" she demanded in the end.

Then, as if she remembered something, she added, "No.

Please don't answer that, Mr. Anshik Dhawan. I have asked the wrong person. You were the first one to break my trust, right?"

He shook his head negatively.

Angry at his denial, she stood up from the bench.

"Thanks for listening to my sob story. And congratulations! It looks like you have attained your goals. Happy for you, but if you don't mind, I must leave, and it is dark."

"I do mind," he retaliated. Ignoring him, she tried to move.

"No, you don't." He dragged her by her hand and stopped her from walking away.

"Sit down. Why did you wish for death?"

"What is there to live for? Don't worry. I will not attempt suicide." She sat back.

"You are not the Ananya I know," he retorted aggressively, not realizing that his hands clasped her shoulders. She took the pain inflicted unconsciously by him.

"You never knew me, Mr. Dhawan."

"Agree. That girl had a fire in her eyes that could never be extinguished."

Moving near, he cupped her cheeks. Staring hard at her honey-brown eyes, he commented sadly, "Gosh, Ananya, I see nothing."

"I have accepted the realities of life. I don't daydream. Anshik, if I have to worry about my next day's meal and a roof over my head, where do I have time to think about my ambitions?" She laughed hysterically, pushing him away with force.

He took some notes from his wallet and stuffed them in her hands.

"You have the money. I want to see the dreams back," he ordered.

For a moment, she was shocked. Time ticked by. "How dare you?"

She flung the money back at him, right in his face.

"My pride and honor are all that I have. To pay for my exam, I worked at a teashop. I went hungry for years to pursue my dreams. And if you believe I'll get money from you, you are damn wrong!"

She got up and began walking away from him, tears streaming down her face.

"Where are you planning to go? Back to your hostel? Or the teashop?" He questioned, as he stood up from the bench. She stopped as his words imparted harsh realities to her mind.

"Anshik, my life is gone, but I am not a charity case."

"I am not giving this money for free. Which world are you in?" he queried incredulously. "Who talked about charity here? Nothing is free in this world. You mentioned earlier that you have one week left in the course. Complete it. I have a job for you."

"Job? Are you kidding me? You own a software company, and I am from a filmmaking background. What do you want me to do?"

"I have opened a new branch today, and we have a cafeteria for the employees, serving tea and coffee. Since you have some experience caring for a teashop, I want you to take charge of the cafeteria."

She contemplated his offer for a moment. God was giving her a second chance, but even before she could start, she was scared that she would not do well. Even if she put in her best efforts, she was absolutely sure that her unluckiness would lead to the downfall of things.

"What is there to think about, Ananya?"

His masculine voice dispelled her negative thoughts. "I'll count to five. The validity of my job offer ends at five."

She turned to him and asked, "Have you gone crazy?"

"1, 2, 3, 4 . . ."

"I accept," she confirmed as she fought against the negativity that threatened to come out.

Smiling, he picked up the money and gave it to her.

"I am paying your first month's salary in advance. Pay your hostel fee and recover your certificates. Collect your offer letter tomorrow and join the office next week. The employees would have moved in by then."

"Why are you helping me out?" she queried, chewing her lips.

"Help? I am repaying you, Ananya."

She had not expected that reply.

"Do you remember our last visit to this temple, Miss Mehta? What did you tell me when I had failed to get a job yet again and was in the same depressed state as you are at present?"

She was quiet.

"I'll repeat what you told me years ago, Ananya. Close the past chapters of your life. Start afresh. START LIVING AGAIN."

A strong gush of wind rang the temple bells. Ananya felt his words echoing around her.

"And I need something in return." He unexpectedly drew her into his arms as her soft face brushed against his broad chest. A gentle breeze blew out of nowhere. Despite the dark clouds, the moon peeked out a little. The atmosphere underwent a complete transformation in a second.

Facing one another after the jerky movement, her hands were against his chest, and she could feel the beat of his heart.

They were hardly an inch apart as he gazed into her honey-dipped eyes. Years melted away.

A bolt of electricity struck them, and Ananya felt warm all over. She could feel his hot breath on her face, and she gasped. That tiny sound ignited his desire.

He steadied her and pushed her bouncy hair back so that he could get an unobstructed view of her face. His gentle touch kept her spellbound, and they lost themselves. With his hands holding her around her hip, she was caught in a snare, which she could not escape.

He gently traced her eyes, and she closed her eyelids as the feelings he evoked transported her to the past, where he meant everything to her. Encouraged by her response, he outlined her cheeks as if he could not help himself.

"Anshik?"

His magnetic eyes argued and commanded her to stay put.

'You are just my friend. I never had that kind of feeling for you.' His cruel declaration from the past came back strong, instilling a wall of fear around her. She knew that he had the power to hurt her again.

'What am I doing?' Her heart chided her for her weakness, bringing her back to her senses, and she moved out of his hold, not meeting his eyes.

Understanding her withdrawal, he said, "Don't overthink, Ananya. Let the past go. I want to see the dream back in your eyes. Think about it."

Thrusting his visiting card into her hands, he let her leave. "It is all up to you."

On that note, he completed the pooja in the temple.

CHAPTER 4

A Fresh Start

You need not wait until your next reincarnation to start a new life. Today is a new day with fresh thoughts. Start living again.

The last week of Ananya's college semester in digital filmmaking went by in a haze. She had consciously avoided meeting Kishore one-on-one, ensuring they didn't exchange words. But on the last day, he caught her right outside the class. With nowhere to go, he forced her to listen to his goading. He smiled, but she realized how fake it was. Why was she not able to figure this out earlier? She chided herself for being gullible.

With his plans all taking off successfully, he dangled his victory in front of her nose.

"Hi, Ananya, nice to see you after my win," he boasted.

"Your win?"

"Come on. Don't be jealous. You should be happy for me. Life isn't always a bed of roses, and things can go wrong. You should be prepared, so don't blame me. It was your fault, not mine," he justified himself.

"By the way, we are beginning our first round of script discussion next week. What are your plans?" He rubbed salt on her wounds.

Irritated with his attitude and query, she ignored his taunt and tried to move away from him, but he blocked her. She held a file in her hands.

"What do you want, Kishore?"

"Now, this is not a way to treat your old friend, right? Act good with me, and I'll throw a few chances at you which come my way."

"I am astounded to see your height of arrogance," she condemned, as a wave of resentment washed over her as she remembered how he had schemed to get her script. With a lunge, he grabbed the file from her hands.

"What are you doing?" she yelled.

"Are you working on a new script?"

He opened her file with vicious intention.

"Stop it," she commanded, which was brushed aside.

The offer letter from TechWarriors caught his attention.

"Wow! This is your future. But what connection do you have with Information Technology?" He frowned, not getting the link.

"Give me my letter, Kishore. You are violating my privacy!"

She tried to grab the file, but he stepped back, increasing the distance between them. He scanned her offer letter swiftly.

"Oh, now I get it. You are about to become a facility supervisor," he mocked. She was furious and retrieved her file.

He scrunched his wide jaw. "Hmm . . . interesting, right? And that, after completing a filmmaking course?" he belittled her.

"And what will you be doing at the office? Mop the floor? Arrange the stationary items in order, or take care of the tea and coffee requirements of the employees?" he ridiculed her.

Shocked at his rudeness, she stepped back.

"Hah, so that is it. You are going to make tea for the employees. I thought you would hit your low, but never this low."

His harsh laughter echoed throughout the entire corridor. Kishore was finally showing his true face without a mask.

"You never loved me, right?" she whispered, shocked at his attitude.

"Oh, my foolish Ananya . . . I portrayed the role of falling in love with you because I needed your incredible scripts."

He looked at his watch, tired of his amusement.

"Okay then, I got to go. Wishing you a bright future as a *chaiwali*."

He wished her well in a tone laced with sarcasm.

*****

Reporting her arrival to the HR manager on her first day, Ananya took charge of the cafeteria in the new building. Anil Dutta, the facility manager for all their Pune offices, welcomed her. Taking her to the cafeteria, he elaborated on her role.

During working hours and a few hours before and after, she had to make sure there was enough milk in the coffee machine. The manager had to know the number of coffee and tea consumed by the employees in a month; she also had to send a report on the same. Also, she had to try out different flavors of coffee and come out with authentic recipes to impress the top management and clients, comprehending their taste. Hence, she had to track their culinary interest.

Gagan and Vaishnavi were part of her team to assist, but she eventually was responsible for ensuring everything was running smoothly at the cafeteria. After welcoming her, Gagan and Vaishnavi went to set up the coffee machines.

"Do we need to serve them?" she asked.

"Not required. The employees are free to use these coffee machines. But you might be required to serve the top officials and our clients during meetings to ensure they sign the contracts."

"I got it, Mr. Dutta."

"Call me Anil. I am hardly a couple of years older than you," he encouraged.

"Alright, Anil." She smiled.

"The cafeteria is all yours, Ananya. I have other work to do. I'll drop in later to see how things are working for you."

"Sure, thanks."

With all the instructions passed on, he left happily.

Ananya knew she needed this job to pay for her basic expenditures, but somehow, her heart was not into it.

She was working closer to the counter on an Excel sheet when Anshik entered the cafeteria and saw her there. Except for a few employees, the cafeteria was free. It was eight in the morning, and people would start coming in by nine.

"Hello, Miss Ananya Mehta. Welcome to TechWarriors. Glad to have you here." He gave her a beaming smile.

Powerful and broad-shouldered in a flawless blue suit,

Anshik oozed confidence as he noiselessly walked toward her in his brown leather shoes. His wavy black hair and shrewd eyes gave him a pirate-like appearance. His tall stance affected her, and she could not contradict that. As she caught his eyes, she felt jittery inside.

Oh God, she behaved like a teenager with a hormonal issue!

But Anshik had the same effect on her even when they were younger.

Don't you dare fall into the same pit again, Ananya,' her proactive brain warned her.

Taking a few seconds to calm herself, she answered, "Hello, Mr. Dhawan. Glad to see you as well," she responded formally to her boss.

Noting her courteous reply, he inquired, "All set for your first day?"

She nodded with little enthusiasm, duly noted by Anshik.

"But I don't see the light in your eyes on the first day," he criticized.

"What is there to get excited about making tea?" she mumbled unintelligibly.

"Sorry, I did not get you." He bent forward to catch her voice.

"What I meant, Mr. Dhawan, is that I am all geared up for my first day." She altered her statement diplomatically.

"Prove it, then."

She frowned, confused.

"As your first task, try out a new flavor of coffee today and bring that to my office in an hour."

He threw the challenge at her and walked out.

"Mr. Dhawan, don't you want your morning coffee?"

"I'll wait for yours."

Recollecting her mother's special recipe, she prepared a coffee with a tint of jaggery. Her first hour at the job was going well. Satisfied with the outcome, she brought the tray from the small kitchen counter and set it close to her laptop to check if she had received a mail from HR. She was supposed to collect her ID card later that day.

After confirming that she had received no such mail, she lifted the resin tray to take it to Anshik's office on the top floor. Anil had told her in the induction session. But a new male coming inside captured her attention.

"Oh gosh, Sandeep *bhaiya*!" she exclaimed.

A familiar but distressed sound reached him. He stood shell-shocked, staring at her. He moved closer to confirm that it was indeed his younger sister, who ran away from home, going against their father.

"It is true," he whispered at the confirmation.

"*Bhaiya*."

His embarrassment showed as he saw her holding a tray of coffee. Wordlessly, he left the cafeteria, not even acknowledging her once.

"No, wait." Her voice was ignored.

She swiftly set the coffee tray down and turned to Gagan and Vaishnavi, who were unpacking a new coffee machine.

"Please take care. I will be back soon."

At their friendly nod, she ran to him.

"Sandeep *bhaiya*, wait, please."

She pleaded grabbing his hand, and caught him close to the elevator. Furious, he shook her hands away.

"What are you doing, Ananya? Stay away!"

"Are you not happy to see me?"

"I would have been if I had not seen you as a server," he admonished.

"No job is nasty, *bhaiya*—"

"Don't call me that ever again. Look where your stupid decision has brought you. Did you fight with papa and leave home to serve tea and coffee?"

"No, I did not."

"What brings you here, then? You intended to make movies. How long has it been since you left the house? Two or three years? I don't recall seeing your name in a single movie or short film."

His queries were reasonable, but she did not have an answer.

"You are a failure, Ananya. Why don't you just be realistic and go back home? Papa might be angry, but he will be pleased once you agree to his plan for the betterment of your life. We are not your enemies."

"I'll not argue with you, *bhaiya*." Her voice was stern and stopped his retort.

He wailed, "I don't get this. Even if you can't do what you dreamed of, what is the necessity of working here as a server, where I work as a technical team lead? I am leading four projects here, and I am ashamed of you."

"I am the facility supervisor here and need the money for my expenses."

"Hmm, no more stars in your eyes. You have become realistic. Welcome back to the world of living," he commented sarcastically.

"*Bhaiya*," she muttered, "don't you see why I have to do this? Our papa made you a successful IT engineer. You don't know the struggles I must go through to maintain a roof over my head."

"If you had married the NRI boy that papa chose, you could have had more than just a roof and food. But you made your choice, Ananya."

"I did!" She nodded.

"Do whatever you want. But don't come near me again." He brushed her off and stepped into the elevator.

*****

Ananya was glad that Sandeep *bhaiya* had settled well in his career. But his harsh words hurt her confidence badly and drained her remaining mental strength. He was a mini replica of her father. To both, it was their way or nothing.

Coming back to her senses, she rushed back to her tray. Knowing Anshik would be waiting, she heated the coffee inside the microwave and carried it to the top floor. There, she noticed a large room with his name on it. Her brain redirected her unconsciously, and she knocked.

"Come in."

With light blue walls, the room was chic, spacious, and airy. Anshik sat behind an enormous table, working on his laptop. The teak bookshelf in the corner enhanced the beauty of the walls. Ceramic flower vases were placed on the other end. The vast window behind provided an aerial view of the city, which was breathtaking.

Anshik observed Ananya. In her embroidered white kurti, she looked gorgeous despite wearing no makeup. Her hair was tied into a messy bun, and small gold hoops adorned her ears. His heart longed to hug her. He had known her for years, yet there was this unbreachable barrier between them, and he knew that he was responsible for that.

With her head bent, her attention was elsewhere.

"Miss Mehta." He could not get her attention.

"Ananya," his voice came out sharp with the second call.

Jolted out of her thoughts, her hands trembled, and hot coffee scalded her hands.

"Ouch!"

"Are you alright?" He ran to her side. He retrieved the tray from her hand and put it on the glass top of the mahogany table.

"What were you thinking of? Have you gone crazy?" he scolded her.

"I . . ." she stammered.

He dragged her to the washbasin in the corner. Holding her hands, he submerged them in the water. Her right hand revealed a red mark despite two minutes under the icy stream.

Shaking his head, he retrieved the first aid box from the last drawer.

"How careless can you get, Ananya?" his tirade continued.

"Stop shouting at me, Mr. Dhawan. It was not intentional. And I am sorry for bringing you trouble," she retaliated, not understanding the concern behind his words.

He frowned and made her sit on the leather chair. He applied some ointment to her burns, attending to them.

"You are not a trouble to me," he told her quietly.

His ointment healed her fingers, and his gentle words were like a soothing balm for her heart. This could quickly become an addiction, and she did not want to invite more trouble into her life.

"Mr. Dhawan . . ."

She tried to pull her hands away. Her resistance made him furious.

"Stop this drama of calling me Mr. Dhawan, Ananya."

"You are my boss."

"Yes, I am. But there was a time when I was more to you than that!"

She gasped as he pulled her closer and leaned into the chair.

"When we kissed, you called me Ansh. Do you remember our kiss, Ananya?"

Caught in his hold, she stared at him.

"Let me know if you have forgotten it. I'll remind you again," he taunted.

CHAPTER 5

Rebuilding Relationships

The best gift you could ever give someone is to make
them smile despite the bad happenings in their life.

Ananya returned to her senses as he reminded her of their kiss—a moment that she would never forget. Her heart issued a red alert, and her body stiffened. She would never fall for his charms again. She had plenty of troubles these days and did not want to add any more to her list, as Anshik was trouble with a capital 'T.'

With fuming anger, she retaliated, "Mr. Dhawan, to you it was never a . . ."

He raised his eyebrows, prompting her to continue.

"I mean . . . for you, it was nothing important. I have a significant memory. If I could recall

43

your exact words, it was something that happened just like that, where you lost yourself momentarily, and it was meaningless."

His previous words still had the power to hurt her.

"But to you, it was not like that, right?" he questioned, probing into her eyes intensely. She backed up a bit to dodge his query and turned back to the washbasin to put her hands back in the water.

Laughing inwardly at her tactics, he asked, "How long will you do that? Your fingers might disappear."

His query agitated her. She stepped on the water spilled beneath the basin without noticing. "Oops!"

Her wail alerted him, and she would have fallen if Anshik had not held her from behind with his muscular arms. With his height, he towered over her.

Her kurti fluttered in the air coming through the window. The cabin door was closed. She had to lift her face to meet his jet-black eyes, and that was a grave mistake, as she drowned in his fiery eyes, set amidst his thick lashes. Her heart pounded at his closeness. His woody perfume taunted her nostrils. Mesmerized, she stood, trapped by his invisible snare, temporarily forgetting the pain in her hands.

With her hair curling on her shoulders toward Anshik, she looked almost ethereal with her classically sculpted face. Though she claimed to be unaffected by his presence, he knew that was not true. Her response excited him and brought out an illicit pleasure he could not deny. With one arm holding her tight, he pushed her hair beside her ears and brought her closer until they were hardly an inch apart.

Ananya's brain instructed her to push him away, yet she stood still. Her legs felt weak, and she could not move.

His lips brushed her forehead, and she felt a bolt of electricity shooting through her.

"Mr.—"

He cut off her words by putting his finger over her lips and felt them trembling with his touch.

"If you call me Mr. Dhawan one more time in private, I'll kiss you, Ananya. Okay?"

With the atmosphere sizzling around them, he stepped back, giving her space to breathe.

She nodded dazedly. What had just happened? What had she agreed to? How could she have almost given in to such a feeling? Her cheeks were red. It was Anshik who had broken their moment of intimacy. A wave of embarrassment swept through her.

He went to his seat, taking the cup of coffee with him.

The first sip took him to the coffee she had made for him during her college days when she had come to his home as his sister's friend. The flavor was perfect.

"Sweet old days," he commented, trying to read her.

"Why are you trying to bring up the past?"

"Why not?" he countered.

"I would not have accepted to work here if I had known that you would rake up the past."

"Do you want to forget?" He gave her a few seconds to think it over.

"Anshik, you urged me to let the past go and move on. I took your advice to heart and am sticking with it. That would be for the best."

Her words broke him, but they were true. He realized that bringing up the past would not get him any brownie points from her. In fact, all the loaded shots were going to backfire on him. He changed the track of their conversation.

"And why do you claim yourself a failure?"

"What else am I?"

He was distraught at hearing her words. The girl he knew was nowhere to be seen.

"Come again. I never expected those words from you."

"But I am a failure."

"This is not the end, Ananya."

She pouted as if she did not care.

He clasped her hand and squeezed it hard from the other side, as if that would bring her back to her senses. She ignored the agony as she shoved his hand away.

"Stop it. Your words will not change the fact that I have lost everything."

"Whatever you have lost can be replaced."

"Easier to say that when you have everything. You can preach to me," she sneered.

"How was I three years ago? Rich and successful? No, Ananya . . . I had nothing. What I have today is all because of my hard work and the sacrifices I made in life."

He was proud of all he had accomplished so far, except for one sacrifice he had to make. But he continued, "You have a new job and a place to stay."

"A new job of making coffee and tea?" she spoke in a derogatory tone as she repeated her brother's words. Somewhere deep inside, it had badly broken her mental state.

"Do you find that degrading?"

She thought for a second, trying her best to forget what Sandeep *bhaiya* had told her. "No, I don't. I need the money. But this is not what I want to do in life. My dreams are different."

"Who is stopping you? The wicked boss?"

"Circumstances . . ."

Angrily, he got off his chair.

"In my perspective, the people who blame the circumstances are losers, Ananya, and you are behaving like one."

"Anshik, I'm exhausted and don't want to argue anymore. And how does that even matter to you?"

"Because my heart wishes to see the older version of the carefree Ananya, the one with hope in her heart and dreams in her eyes."

"Why? So that you can play with her feelings again?"

The moment the words were out, she regretted it.

He might have been her friend once upon a time, but now he was her boss. And if he threw her out of this job, she knew that she had nowhere to go.

Ananya's words hit him hard. He knew that he had hurt her in the past. But seeing her in this state made him helpless. His only priority was to bring back the lost Ananya.

"I am—"

"Keep your sorry to yourself," he blasted.

"You might think that this job is menial for you. But remember that there are many who wish that they were in your seat now."

His authoritative tone did the trick. He was sick of lending a soft hand with his advice, and at present, she required a shaking, and he would do that if it helped her.

"Lose yourself for all I care and drown in sorrow without realizing that everything is in your hands only. It does not matter to me personally, but I find your lack of enthusiasm a turnoff, Ananya . . . as a boss."

His tirade continued, "You can destroy yourself by wallowing in self-pity all the time. But I warn you. Don't do that at the office. Am I clear?"

Within a second, all traces of the person she knew were gone. Only the boss was left.

She nodded without looking into his eyes.

"Be yourself, Ananya."

"Don't worry, Mr . . . Anshik. I will do my job to perfection. How is the jaggery coffee?" Her pride came to her rescue.

He smiled. "I would like to see this enthusiasm exhibited everywhere."

"I will. Who said I would not? My personal life has no connection to this office," retorted Ananya.

She wanted to earn her keep.

"Anil asked me to check if it is okay to serve this flavor of coffee to our clients from Foodzie who are visiting us today."

He didn't give her a single glance as he returned to his seat.

"Yes, please." He lost interest in her as his laptop caught his attention. What should have been a relief to Ananya now disturbed her, as she wished they had more time together.

'What is wrong with me? Why am I longing for my punishment?'

She pushed her thoughts away and questioned, "Anything else, boss?"

"Nothing."

She was so frustrated that she wanted to stomp her feet on the ground in frustration. She turned to go while trying to remain calm.

"Ananya?" She halted at the door at his call.

"Kavya wants to meet you. She has invited you to come home. She will come on the fifth of next month."

"But—"

"I am your villain from the past, right? What did my sister do? Before you deny her invitation, let me show her message."

He scrolled through his messages. "Look at this."

She took his mobile and read the content.

'*Oh my God, is Ananya joining our office? I am longing to meet her, bhaiya. It has been years. Please . . . tell her to come home. I miss her badly.*'

Thoughts of Kavya made her smile. "I would love to."

"Fine then. I will text you my new address. Keep it handy."

"Is she not staying with you?"

He shook his head. "She is a successful model now. She has set up her base in Mumbai. You would have known if you had kept in touch with her at least."

She ignored his last taunt.

"I'm happy for her success. Will you . . ."

She paused, realizing what she was about to ask.

"Will I be there? How does it matter to you?" He threw the ball back at her.

Ignoring his taunt, she affirmed, "It doesn't matter at all. I'll come and meet her."

*****

Two weeks passed with no disruption. Ananya settled well into her job. Though she had not seen Anshik after the first day, his harsh advice had made her think. Her heart longed to believe that the terrible phase she was going through was temporary and that she had to try again.

"Do you think it is that easy with your so-called bad luck, Ananya?" her brain contemplated.

"I agree that it is difficult. But I can try again," her heart countered.

"So that you can fail yet again and be the laughingstock of the town!"

"Will I fail once more?" Self-doubt crept up.

"Come on, be realistic girl, and stick to reality. How many times have you tried so far? Can you even count?"

"Many times . . ."

"Right. And what happened? Look where you are now!"

"But, I want to be a filmmaker." Her heart longed to attain her dreams.

"Like papa said, stop chasing wild dreams and hold on to what you have now."

Wiping her dreams along with her tears, she somehow accepted reality.

She looked at her watch. It was time. She had packed fresh-made jaggery coffee in a flask. She had received a mail in the morning from Mr. Anil to join their boss, Mr. Anshik Dhawan, who was about to visit a big client, the CEO of TriggerGreen, the company that produced fertilizers. The meeting was happening at their other branch, and the agenda was to improve their existing software.

Anshik and other officials would do the talking, and she was supposed to serve the best of her coffee and keep them happy. Although they had a facility manager over there, Anshik had insisted to Anil that her version of jaggery coffee had made the mark when the clients had visited their office earlier, and she had to be there to serve her delicacy to get the credit.

She met him in the basement parking lot. Standing close to his black-sporty Benz car, he looked classy in an immaculately tailored pale green mohair suit and an ivory silk shirt with a red tie. He looked striking, and his body had an element of lethal power. She felt small, as his height and breadth dwarfed her. There was an aura of arrogance surrounding him, which she thought suited him well.

Anshik held his breath as she walked toward him. She was neither too thin nor obese with her curvy body. Dressed in a red cotton sari with her hair tied up into a ponytail, she appeared formal yet feminine. The white stone studs on her ears went well with her cut-out black shoes, and he felt as if he could frame her into a picture and hang this moment in his room forever. Her lopsided smile bewitched him.

"Good morning, Anshik," she said, coming to him with her courtesy wish.

He smiled. "All ready?"

"Yes, I have got my flask. I'll not have time to do it over there," she told him apologetically.

"That is okay, Ananya. I am not an ogre of a boss to demand an on-spot delivery."

She laughed. "I have to give you that compliment. Anyway, you are not my boss. Mr. Anil is. You are way up my hierarchy to be my boss."

It led to a frown on his face. "Come, let us go. I have to stop somewhere else as well."

His friendly banter broke her wall of defense. *'Be careful, Ananya. A charming Anshik is more dangerous.'*

She repeated the words internally. She was about to climb into the backseat when she noted that Anshik had opened the front door for her.

He lifted his eyebrows as if daring her to sit at the back.

"Are you scared to sit with me?"

Closing the back door with a bang, she came to the front and got into his car. "No, why should I be?"

"I thought maybe the feelings from the past were catching up with you."

She wanted to retaliate by saying that it was nothing of the sort, but Anshik bent into the car and closed her mouth with his hands.

"Please don't. Allow a man to have some dreams."

Ananya did not want to react, but she could not stop her blush from spreading across her face. She did not understand his behavior. He was the one who had thrown her out of his life. What was he trying to achieve now?

But her heart did not listen to her reasoning. It pounded heavily at his touch. Her fingers touched his hand to remove his hold on her lips, but they stuck to his as if they were glued. Time appeared to freeze as their feelings threatened to loom large.

To Anshik, it was a beautiful form of torture. He could feel her lips on his palm. He wanted to drink the honey from her eyes. She was all he needed, but this was neither the place nor the time for it. With a sigh of regret, he took his hands away and went to his driving seat.

Coming to her senses, she made a play at adjusting the pleats of her sari, avoiding his eyes. That held his attention. Her fair skin glowed against the fresh morning wind that rushed through the partly opened door. Her face crinkled as she strained to avoid him consciously, but all he could see were the dimples that dominated her oval face. And he knew that he had already fallen into it and would never come out of it. He let out a sigh of regret. He had to keep his feelings of love and desire under control.

It took a couple of minutes for Ananya to break their silence.

"Anshik, you told me that we need to stop somewhere in between, right?"

"Yes. There is a small farm beside our head office. We need to go there to understand the farming process better before we meet Mr. Dinesh Patil, the head of TriggerGreen. In this way, we'll have better suggestions for software improvement and automation."

"Wow, that is a productive idea," she appreciated.

"Yes, I know. But I am not sure if anyone will be there on the farm right now. We could not check the farmer's availability. He was not there yesterday."

"Hope he is there today," she told him, covering her earlier embarrassment. With their earlier moment haunting them, silence dominated their drive.

Anshik parked his car outside the farm after fifteen minutes, despite the heavy traffic. Ananya stepped out of the car and was shocked to see the sight that awaited them.

"Anshik, come out quick. Look there!" she yelled.

The urgency in her tone made him halt the car even before parking it correctly. Leaving everything behind, they ran toward the farmer to stop him.

He was busy tying a threaded rope around his throat.

"*Bhaiya*, stop. Don't do it," he commanded.

CHAPTER 6

Ups and Downs

Ups and downs make your life. 'Ups' push you up and 'downs' push you up as well, if you don't allow the 'downs' to overrule you.

Anshik held the muddy feet of the old man, who was on the verge of ending his life. "Stop this, sir."

"No, I'll not," he attempted to resist, pushing away his hands. But with his old age, he could never match Anshik's strength.

Anshik pulled the elderly man down by holding onto his feet. His shorts were muddy with dirt. Shirtless, he could see traces of smeared dust all over his shoulders. Despite his age, his hands and legs appeared weathered and showed traces of hard work. "Leave me. I want to die," he wailed.

"No one in this world has the right to throw away their life, no matter how much they want to."

Anshik's words came out harshly.

"I have nothing to live for," the man countered.

Anshik's eyes met Ananya's. Those were the exact words she had spoken at the temple that day. Feeling uncomfortable under his stare, she bent her head to avoid his complaining look. Dwelling in his sorrow, the old man overlooked this by-play.

"Stop saying that. It is a sin to give up on life," he growled impatiently.

"What else can I do? Look there."

He showed his field of *Sevanti* flowers. Half of the plants were uprooted, while the other half were coated partly with some black powder.

Anshik and Ananya gasped.

"I had rented these two acres of land and planted the seeds of *Sevanti*. Even though I used the best fertilizer available, I could not stop this catastrophe. All of the harvest has become contaminated, and the only thing I can do is destroy the blossoms. God! You cannot imagine my pain when I ripped the flowers."

His voice was shaky as he broke down. He wiped the dirty tears away from his wrinkled cheeks and continued, "And I borrowed money for all of this."

He grabbed a handful of sand and let it flow through his fingers. With agony engulfing him, he thumped his field hysterically and sobbed.

Anshik put his hands on him in support while he unloaded his sorrows.

"I have lost everything. With an enormous debt hanging over my head, what can I do? You tell me."

Realizing that the old man was prompting him for his name, he told him, "Anshik."

"Yes, tell me, Anshik. Even at seventy-two, I tried my best. But I should have known that I am the son of the Goddess of bad luck, and she never abandons me. I've been trying for years to improve my life, but I have grown weary and am now sick of it. I should have been realistic and refrained from dipping into my savings."

Forgetting his audience, he was glad to pour his heart out. It was Ananya's turn to glare at Anshik. "See, this is what I said. Life is never easy with all the bad luck." She communicated through her eyes.

"Instead, I craved for more. I believed I could do better in my life. Hence, I used up all my earnings and borrowed money to pursue my dreams of becoming a great farmer. And look where it has led me now."

Ananya voiced her feelings. "Sir, I can understand what you are going through."

With his white beard and mustache, he looked older than seventy-two.

Anshik glared at them both. "This is not the time for self-pity. And with all your years of wisdom, you can't deny that. What made you decide to make the extreme move? Why did you not ask for help, sir?"

"Help for what? To pay back the money I borrowed? Even if someone was ready to help, how would I pay that person back? I have nothing."

Out of desperation, he threw the blackened flower lying at his side.

"So, you'll kill yourself and escape like a coward?"

"It's easier for you to talk about hope, young man. Many farmers go through this phase, leaving them nothing. I must die . . ., though I don't want to . . .," he wailed.

"Sir, I neither have the age nor your experience of life to advise you. But I can repeat our ancient Hindu scriptures. Suicide is the biggest sin of all."

He turned to him with regret. "Don't you have one reason to live?"

"Grandpa," a boy of around thirteen years ran to him.

"I waited for you. You promised to come home for breakfast," the cute boy complained.

"Did you not have your food yet?" the grandpa asked.

"When have I ever eaten without you, grandpa?" The boy's query was out of love.

Anshik's eyes caught the old man's as they demanded, "Is he not a reason enough?"

"Yes, how did I forget him? His parents are dead. He has no one except me," he muttered, giving up his pathetic idea of suicide.

"There you have your answer. Sometimes complicated layers of emotion cloud our vision, preventing us from making rational choices."

The old man hugged his grandson, glad to be with him again.

"I have to live, Anshik . . . for my grandson's sake."

Anshik nodded in affirmation.

"Do you know, young man? People don't plan suicide. They simply go ahead with a momentary aberration in desperation."

He continued, "After seeing my grandson's face, I regret my decision badly. I will borrow or do whatever it takes to provide a better life for this boy. He should not suffer for my mistakes."

"Are you not 72-years-old? Is it not too late to get back what you have lost?" Anshik teased.

"72 is the new 22." He laughed gruffly.

Anshik clasped his hands. "Hold on to that laughter and the thought, sir . . . When you laugh during the tough times, everything else disappears. Don't worry; I'll help you out with a loan. This is my card."

His eyes were full of gratitude. "Do you really mean it?"

He nodded, taking in his happiness.

"Thank you so much. May you get what you long for soon," he blessed.

And Anshik knew for what or for whom his mind longed. But will she ever understand him?

*****

Relieved and happy about the old man, Anshik and Ananya returned to the car.

"Anshik, we have missed the meeting."

"Yes, but I don't regret it. Nothing is more important than humans," he remarked. He called his personal assistant and informed him about his delay.

Cutting off the call, he said, "Good news! The client has agreed to reschedule the meeting for next week."

Ananya smiled. "Great then. Let us get back to our office."

The car tires screeched as Anshik hit the brakes on his car.

"What happened?"

"Get down, Ananya."

"But this isn't our office."

"How observant you are," he teased.

She glared. "We can go back to the office after tasting your coffee. I need some time to unwind after the morning incident."

On that note, he walked into the City Park. Ananya followed him while carrying the flask. "He has gone crazy," she muttered, shaking her head.

"I heard you, Ananya," he warned and raised his hands light-heartedly, as if he were about to hit her. She took a few steps back, not noting the cobblestones on the road, and slipped.

Anshik swiftly caught her in his arms. He laughed and looked into her chocolate-dripping eyes before saying, "Swooning in my arms has become your habit, Ananya. From now on, considering your safety, I'll carry you, always locking you to me."

Pushing him a little, she proclaimed, "I can save myself, Mr. Hero, and even if I fall, you are too old to carry me."

She taunted him, and Anshik tugged her gently and made her sit on the stone bench.

"This is the first time I have seen you laugh, Ananya, after a long time . . ."

She held her breath.

"If a 72-year-old man can find the will to survive and fight for his life, don't you think you can do the same, Ananya?"

She had the feeling of being physically smacked. He was right.

"You might feel that you have lost everything, Ananya. But you have not. All you require is one reason to fight back and hold on."

A vision of her being a filmmaker flashed by, and a shot of happiness coursed through her. She nodded dazedly, and her mind started churning.

"You have been wallowing in the well of self-pity. And I don't blame you. Everyone goes through such a phase.

But what matters is how you come out of it. It is time to break that phase of darkness, Ananya."

He cupped her cheeks as she turned to him. They stood in silence as he gave her time to grasp what he was talking about.

A wave of gratitude pushed her to give him a bear hug. She had needed him all her life. Where was he all this time?

A genuine bond of affection captivated them, as her mind unburdened itself from her recent troubles.

"*Wah,* I did not expect that."

"Thank you," she whispered as she got clarity. The haze in her mind disappeared. She could think rationally as the years faded.

She could clearly see the road to her professional dreams, and even her trauma seemed to vanish.

Anshik's support had proved that he was her best friend, as he had claimed three years ago. He was by her side even today, adding value to their friendship. Ananya sighed at her mistaken belief. She was the one who had read more into their tender relationship and had confused everything from the start, getting it all wrong as 'love'.

There was no point in holding a grudge against him for her misunderstanding years ago. He had taken a clear stance earlier, and she should have respected that. And she had to do the same now and set a clear-cut boundary between them.

If not, she was in grave danger of repeating her mistake of falling for him again. Even a glance at his mesmerizing eyes would lure her into the trap of love.

She was emotionally scared that expressing her love for him would make him leave her like last time. She wanted him in her life forever. *'Stay friendly, Ananya . . . keep your heart safe. That is what he wants. Don't threaten him with your unwarranted feelings.'*

"I don't need your appreciation, Ananya."

His gruff voice interrupted her thoughts.

Anshik crossed his fingers and wished hard that Ananya would realize his feelings for her and read what his eyes said. Her gratitude wasn't enough for him. He needed more than that. But he could not confess what had happened in their past and why he had pretended to be just a friend. He chose not to create a negative image of his mother since he believed her intentions were right, despite her promise that she took from him.

While Anshik wished fervently that Ananya would realize his love for her, she was embroiled in her world of thoughts. She failed miserably to read between the lines.

"Years ago, when you told me we were just friends, I felt degraded, and it hurt me badly. But now I understand."

"Do you?"

"I confess that I made an error and misinterpreted our relationship. I appreciate how great of a friend you are now as you were then. "

He gasped. This was not what he expected.

She badly wanted to convince him that they were just friends to please him, not realizing that she was doing vice versa.

"Love and friendship are interconnected," he stressed.

She laughed a little forcefully, hiding her despair. "Are they?"

He frowned. Seeing his grimace, she did her best to keep their relationship friendly.

"But now I am thankful we did not complicate our relationship further."

Astonished, he demanded, "Why?"

"When I look back, I realize how young I was. There are still many areas for me to explore and experience today."

That was yet another reason that he had to leave her. He nodded in silence. The idea of her accepting their breakup and moving on did not sit well with him. He wanted to shake her and demand, "Are you mad? Can't you sense what I feel for you? I had no other choice. I was kidding myself when I said you were just my friend. We are meant to be forever, stupid Anu."

The unspoken words triggered a melancholic feeling as his emotions tightened his heart, but she failed to notice it.

She continued, "Love and friendship . . . they are different, Anshik. I get it now. I have told you about Kishore. Despite saying he loved me, he stole my script from me. How can you do that to someone you love?"

"Then it was never love in the first place," he argued, relieved that it had been nothing more than a disillusion.

"But with you, it is different, Anshik. And I am happy that our friendship has stood the test of time. You are helping after my fall, unlike love, which backstabbed me cunningly."

"You are confused, Ananya. Don't overthink," he pleaded.

She inched closer to him. "My vision is clear. You have removed the cobwebs of ignorance that covered my eyes. I have dreams to chase, happiness to find, and I need to mend my broken life."

She stretched her hands. "And will you stay as my friend, like always, and help me find all the things that I have lost?"

He wanted to scream and shout that he wanted to be her lover and not just a friend. But looking at the excitement in her puppy eyes, he shook hands with her.

"Oh dear, things are changing for me. Thank you, Anshik."

She hugged him exuberantly, and he ruffled her hair gently.

Pouring coffee from the flask into the paper cups, she passed it to him, taking one for herself.

"After a long time, I am looking forward to the next day in my life, Anshik."

He smiled despite her declaration of their relationship status. At least she was back in the land of the living. He would take it from there.

"Thank you for that."

"I am sick of your thanks, Ananya. That is not something I want."

He stayed grim as they drank their coffee in silence.

"Did I do something wrong?" she enquired innocently, observing his anger. She thought he would be pleased as she had openly acknowledged him as her friend, as he had wanted years ago.

'Yeah, you did. You friend-zoned me just like that.'

He did not utter those words loudly. But inside, he was fuming. Did Ananya lose her feelings for him along the way? But this was not the right time to discuss it. She was ready to put things on track, ignoring other factors that could weigh her down. Raking up old love stories or a declaration of his feelings would not help. He had to wait for her, and he did not know how long. But one thing was for sure.

"Ananya . . ."

"I would walk alongside you no matter what." His tone was sincere.

"Thank you, my friend."

If Ananya referred to him as her friend one more time, he was sure he would kiss her, stopping those words in her mouth before they were out. But he had to hold himself, as he was the reason behind the same.

CHAPTER 7

Dealing with
Emotional Loss

*Painful, irreplaceable losses can take you down,
punching you with emotional weight. It is difficult
to heal these scars, yet you need to learn to live
with them. Accept the fact that life is unfair at
times.*

A week passed by. Ananya had to wait another week to meet her old buddy, Kavya. Her heart longed to see her. She doubted if she was excited to see Kavya or her brother, Anshik? She had not seen him much at the office. Their company had secured a deal with the fertilizer company—TriggerGreen—and he had been busy with that.

'*Come on, only a week ago, you declared openly that he was your best friend. Don't confuse your feelings again. Be a good girl, Ananya,*' she instructed herself sternly and took the elevator.

She stepped out to see Anil and Anshik seated next to each other in the cafeteria. The top of the resin table before them was elegant, adorned with pebbles and flowing blue liquid resembling a sea. It appeared elegant and was surrounded by glass walls, yet the gaps allowed sunlight to stream in. She placed the tray of freshly brewed coffee on their table with a smile. Gagan and Vaishu were busy cleaning the coffee machines.

Anil pretended to use a microphone to announce her entry and exclaimed, "Here comes the stunning lady who manages the cafeteria brilliantly."

"Stop it, Anil," she chided playfully, tapping his hands. Anil caught her hands in a friendly manner.

Anshik observed their easy banter with a flicker of curiosity. A subtle unease settled within him. As he realized he was holding her hand, a surge of discomfort swept over him, his mind racing with irrational thoughts.

What if it meant something more than friendship?'

He growled inwardly, the possibility gnawing at him.

Anil queried, "Am I saying something wrong? She is gorgeous, right, Anshik?"

In a knee-length frilly white gown, she appeared like an angel who had descended from the sky. A black belt and shoes completed her outfit. Her smile brought out the dimples lurking inside, and her lush, pink lips would tempt any red-blooded man.

He agreed with irritation. "Better leave her hands. She is embarrassed."

Anil dropped her hand and agreed, "You are right, boss."

Ananya observed Anshik. He was dressed in a round-necked white T-shirt with blue jeans, keeping it casual on a

Friday. His shades hung from the front opening, and he was attractive enough to capture the attention of all the women in the cafeteria. He exuded raw power and masculinity, and it had the potential to disturb her badly.

"Her coffee is to die for. If God asked me my last wish before my death, I would ask for a cup of coffee made by Ananya," Anil proclaimed dramatically.

"If you want to have a coffee, get it from the machine," the CEO scowled.

Ananya could not help but notice his odd behavior.

"Tasting her coffee and judging its taste is a part of my job, boss."

"Fine, then share your review with her and send me the report," Anshik advised moodily and left the cafeteria abruptly.

"But . . ." Anil wanted to know why his boss had changed his plan suddenly. They still had things to discuss, and his input always helped.

"What has got into him?" his bewilderment showed in his query.

"Let me figure that out," Ananya volunteered.

She disregarded the strange but judgmental look that Anil gave in return. She caught hold of Anshik as he was about to storm into his room.

"Anshik, please wait."

He ignored her call. She stepped in before he could close his door.

Catching hold of his arms, she enquired, "What happened?"

He did not reply, but she could sense his anger.

"You promised to continue our friendship, right?"

He looked at her as if she spoke the language of aliens.

"What has that got to do now?"

"Then answer me! Communication is the key to any relationship."

"Is it? You have sorted your feelings and labeled what we have got as 'friendship'? But what is Anil to you? Your love?"

She left his arms and frowned. "He is my colleague."

"Seriously?" He let out a sigh of anger and gripped her hands.

"Take a note, Ananya, flirting is strictly forbidden at the office."

"Flirting? Who was flirting with whom?" she inquired, perplexed.

"Who else? You! Don't play dumb." He tugged her close as jealousy took him over.

"What are you complaining about?"

"Anil was flirting with you. Am I wrong?"

"This question does not even deserve an answer, Anshik."

"Playing with your fingers and complimenting you is permitted for all men at the office. Is that so?"

"I don't have to answer the queries that invade my personal space. Definitely not to my friends."

"But you are answerable to the head of this office."

"Okay, Mr. Anshik Dhawan. I did not flirt with Anil. Even if I do, it should not matter to you, and I'll ensure that it does not disturb my work."

They stood against each other as if they were in the middle of a major war.

"This is it, Ananya. I have lost my patience. Do you recollect what I told you last time?"

Her face was flushed with anger. He pushed her against the door while holding one of her arms and momentarily locking her.

"You called me Mr. Anshik Dhawan, and I told you that if you do that in private one more time, I'll kiss you."

"No."

She put her hands against his muscular chest to stall him and realized that he was warm and mad all over.

"Ansh . . ." her nervousness betrayed her voice, yet she stayed within the circle of his arms that snaked around her. She realized that her heart was not in tandem with her rational thoughts as it pounded erratically. His nearness made her blush, and butterflies took over her.

'Move out . This will never work out. You are just a friend to him.'

She ignored the warning from her brain. Anshik's eyes grazed the sweetness of her lips, and she could sense his desire for her. Her gaze tangled with his with a craving she could not ignore.

He could sense her dilemma. Before she could give in to that and move away, he placed his hands on the back of head and pulled her face toward him. He drowned willingly into her sensual eyes and wished that this moment would last forever.

Slipping his hand into her silky ponytail, he placed his lips on her forehead and felt her shudder with her pupils dilated.

"Anu," he called her name in wonder.

Tracing his lips along the line of her eyebrows, he stroked her cheeks with his fingers. Her heart hammered, and she could hear a rushing sound with the intimacy of the moment. She almost stopped breathing, waiting for him to continue. Her knees went weak, and she would have fallen if not for the hold he had on her. His hot breath softly played on her skin, and she was lost when his mouth brushed hers tentatively. The moment was shattered as they heard someone knocking on the door. He hesitated for a painful second but moved her out of the way.

Ananya panicked. How could she have allowed him to kiss him like that after announcing him as her friend? She had broken the boundary, and it would be hard to play by her rules, going forward. How pathetic can she get? She let out her breath deeply to calm herself. But she was not thinking rationally. If she had, then she would have wondered why Anshik, being a 'friend', had crossed that boundary.

Anshik gave her a few seconds to recover from their moment. Her face appeared flushed, and he did not want anyone to know what had happened within his room. It was special, and it had to stay only between them. He took his rightful place in his leather chair.

Ananya hurriedly moved to the other corner and sat on the other side of the desk, playing with a few files.

"Come in," Anshik called bossily.

It surprised Ananya to see her brother, Sandeep, walking in.

"Mr. Anshik, sorry to barge in, but I heard Ananya is here."

"Yes. Why do you need to meet her?"

"*Bhaiya*." She stood up.

Anshik was stunned. He knew Ananya had a brother, but he never knew that he worked at his office.

"I have been looking for you all around."

"Why?" she panicked.

Because she knew that until and unless something was wrong, he would never come looking for her.

"Oh sis," he cried.

"What is wrong?"

"Ma . . ."

"What happened to her?" Her voice trembled with anxiety.

"She is no more . . ."

"No!" screamed Ananya. Her wail shattered the men in the room.

"Papa called now, and I came running to you."

"Tell me you are lying, *bhaiya*."

"I wish I could."

"She was fine last month. But ever since you visited her recently, she had fallen sick."

"Oh God . . ."

"Why did you meet her?" he demanded arrogantly.

She did not reply.

"Why?" He pulled her forcefully toward him.

"I needed money," she whimpered.

"Don't you have any shame? Papa was right then. You killed her!"

"What are you saying?"

"She was worried about you, Ananya."

He tugged her away from him. She hit the vase nearby and fell.

Anshik rushed to her. "Are you mad? She is your sister," he shouted at Sandeep.

"I wish I never had a sister like her. She is a constant source of suffering for my papa, and now I have lost my ma because of her," he criticized.

"I know that you are in pain. But that does not give you any right to speak to her this way. She is also in the same state as you are," Anshik cautioned him sternly, to stop his tirade.

Not able to vent out his anger on her with his boss on her side, Sandeep threatened, "That is okay. I don't want to talk to her ever. A word of warning, Ananya. Don't come to the funeral. Papa does not want you there. And I don't want you to hurt him. If I see you there, I'll not be responsible for my own actions."

With that reproving note, he stormed out of the office. Ananya was still lying on the floor, where she had fallen after getting hit against the vase.

Anshik tried to lift her, lending his hand, but she did not budge. Hence, he squatted close to her, to meet her eyes levelly, drenched with tears of agony.

"Why, Anshik? Why should I be hit by everything bad in life?" She sobbed pitifully. Her miserable feelings threatened to break out, and she held his T-shirt and demanded an answer.

"Anu, it is not like that."

Her tears and pain impacted his heart, and his eyes clouded with tears by just looking at her.

"I can't see you cry, Ananya. Please don't," he wanted to plead.

Softly, he brushed her tears away, but she could not stop the salty tears that rolled ceaselessly against her cheeks.

She rambled on. "She was the only soul in my life who supported me and cared for me . . . though she did not dare to stand against papa."

He pushed the lock of her hair that veiled her face behind her ears, allowing her to pour her agony out.

"And that was enough for me, Anshik."

She buried her face in his knees.

"To know that she loved me was enough. I demanded nothing from her."

She moaned regretfully, with her tears drenching his pants.

Suddenly, she lifted her head. "I asked her for money, Anshik. Did I put her in a state of worry and kill her like Sandeep *bhaiya* said?"

"No, please don't think that way. They are angry with you and need a scapegoat to take out their anger."

"No, Anshik . . . I need her. I need my ma." She wept.

"Stop crying."

In her distressed state, she did not notice that Anshik was also crying for her. Her tears troubled him greatly and ripped his heart. He would do anything in the world to stop her from crying.

"How can I not? I have lost my mother," she complained.

"I get it, alright. But will your tears bring her back to life?"

She looked at his face as if taking his words in.

"Yes, nothing is going to bring her back."

Anshik continued smoothing out her hair, trying to soothe her anguish.

She tried to get up but faltered, and Anshik held her, breaking her fall.

She buried her face in his chest and sobbed like a baby without realizing what she was doing. He hugged her, taking in her sorrow, extending his moral support.

"Let your sorrows out, Ananya. I'll be there for you." He kept repeatedly murmuring those reassuring words in her ears, unsure if they even reached her. He kept her in his hold till her sobs died down.

She tried to move away when she realized she had spoilt his clothes with tears. Uncertain about her feelings, Anshik pushed her slightly and made her sit on the chair.

Pouring a glass of water from the jug on the table, he passed it to her.

"Here, have some."

"No," she denied.

"YES."

Realizing that he would not leave her until she drank it, Ananya gulped down the contents of her glass.

"I miss her, Anshik," she reiterated.

He tightened his reassuring grip on her hands. She jumped away like a scalded cat suddenly.

"Anshik, do you remember what you told me earlier?" He frowned.

"Whatever I have lost so far is replaceable, and I could earn back if I put in my efforts, right?"

"Yes."

"And I agreed with you. I wanted to try again despite my failures. But now I have lost my mother. How could I even think about replacing her?"

"What are you talking about?"

"I am bad luck personified, Anshik. Just as I was ready to take control of my life again, this is what fate throws at me. And I am scared, Anshik . . . without her, I am nothing."

"Ananya, don't think when emotions are overruling you. Give it some time."

She did not heed his advice.

"What is the point of fighting against the odds in life when I have no one with me?"

Anshik hit his head in frustration, turning to the other side.

'How do I get her back on track? Why is fate pulling her legs despite her efforts to do better? How much more can she bear? But don't worry, Ananya, whatever happens, I'll always be with you. We will fight this together.'

CHAPTER 8

Blocker from the Past

*Losses from the past should never block the highway
to your future. Derive your strength from the pain
to cross the obstacles and move forward.*

Three months passed, and Anshik gave Ananya some private space and ensured that he did not disturb her mourning. After all, she had lost her mother. Initially, she had taken a few days off, as she was not in the right frame of mind for office work. She had not visited Kavya as planned, taken over by the loss, which had traumatized her. Even now, she interacted little at the office and appeared frozen twenty-four cross seven, as if she was happy to be inside the ice shell.

Anshik got up with those thoughts about Ananya on Saturday. But she had to move on. She had to realize that time never stops, and no matter what happens, life still functions. He used Kavya as his trump card to assist Ananya. He would not sit back and watch his dear girl flounder in her life.

Hence, his sister had spoken to Ananya over the phone last week and had begged her to visit them for a change of mind. Though she did not feel like socializing, Ananya accepted the invite out of courtesy for a friend she had not seen for a long time.

It was hardly five in the morning, and he went for his usual jog. It was not the sound of an alarm that woke him, though. An exhilarating feeling gripped him in the early hours, and his eyes refused to sleep further. Ananya would come home to meet his sister. He stayed in a huge penthouse at Shivaji Nagar, Pune. At the rear of the house were the servant quarters. A fish-shaped pool and a lush green lawn added to the elegance of the house's other corner. The cobblestones acted as a barrier between the lawn and the home. They had ample space for a walk within the compound wall. The head of the security team, Mr. Aryan Hegde, wished him as he came out of the CCTV room at the front.

"Good morning, sir. You are up early," he wished.

"Morning, Aryan. Yes, planning to do some morning workout today," he confirmed.

"Great going, sir," he encouraged.

Anshik had to spend his excessive energy, which stubbornly refused to leave his body, anticipating Ananya's arrival in the evening. Scolding himself for counting the hours, he could not explain his enthusiasm over her arrival. He only hoped she had recovered a little from her mother's death.

*****

Ananya walked in sharply at six in the evening. Mrs. Sheela Dhawan, Anshik's mother, greeted her warmly.

"Welcome, my dear girl. I'm glad to see you after a long time. We missed you much," she welcomed her. Her warm words came out of guilt, which had consumed her. Though it had all been for good, she knew that she was the reason her son broke off despite being crazy about her. She had not wanted that craziness to disturb him at an age when he had not yet settled.

At the helm of his success now, Sheela did not find any reason to disturb them. She wanted to play cupid in their relationship, and she was sure there could never be a better pair for Anshik other than Ananya. She had seen her taking care of him on multiple occasions.

Mr. Ankush Dhawan gave her a fatherly hug.

"Come in, Ananya. We all missed you. Didn't we, Anshik?"

Before Anshik could reply, Kavya crushed her with a tight embrace.

"Hey Anu, I never thought that I'd meet you again. Where were you all these days? How dare you leave me all alone with my sour brother? How are you? And I missed you terribly. Not only me—"

Anshik cut her ramblings short.

"Come in, Ananya. Kavya is going to bombard you with tons of questions. Be prepared." He laughed.

"And Ananya is just coming out of her ordeal, so let us not tax her brain with sentiments, Kavya," he instructed his sister.

"Yeah, Anu. I've heard about your mom. We are deeply sorry for your loss. Don't worry. We are here for you," she uttered her words of apology with genuine regret.

"Thanks, Kavya."

"Join us for some coffee, Kavya," invited Mrs. Sheela.

Dressed in a contrasting dark blue patterned salwar top with a red bottom, Ananya had let her hair free today. She was not in the mood to do an elaborate hairstyle. Her red *dupatta* fluttered around her neck. She had no makeup on her face except for some lip-gloss and wore a simple pearl stud. Anshik could see dark circles under her eyes projecting her sleepless nights of sorrow, though she tried to hide that with a little smile.

They all sat in the living room, and Anshik took his place beside her on the sofa. Kavya sat on his other side and whispered. "You look handsome, bro. Don't worry. You make a perfect pair," she teased.

Anshik stared at her. "Shut up, Kavya," he muttered. But that did not halt her.

"And, *bhaiya*, you have a worn dark blue T-shirt as well. Your wavelengths sync perfectly."

"If you do not stop this nonsense, I will lift you and toss you outside," he threatened.

"I know you will not do that," she tugged his shoulders and leaned on him.

Though Ananya could not hear the conversation, she noticed the loving gesture between Kavya and Anshik. While she was happy for them, she missed her brother badly. During her childhood, she had shared such a rapport with Sandeep. But ever since she left home, he seemed intent on considering her his enemy.

'Probably, I could share the same rapport with Anshik someday.'

'But definitely not as my brother, though.'

Controlling her internal musing, she struggled to keep her face blank.

'*Where are these thoughts coming from?*' She frowned at her thoughts.

'*With no one by my side, I long for someone to show some love. And what is this making me? A pathetic wimp?*'

With harsh self-criticism, she sighed as the maid came in with coffee on a tray and served them in transparent crystal mugs.

"Thanks, Sharda. It smells lovely," complimented Sheela.

"Thank you, Sheela *ji*. I have also made some *pakoras* as you had asked. I will bring that, too." She went in with a smile, happy with the compliment.

"Have your coffee, Ananya. Sharda's coffee is too good to miss, and it can be the best medicine for any sorrow," Kavya advised her friend.

They tried to distract her and kept her occupied with other stories. The Dhawan family made extra efforts to make her feel comfortable, which made her miss her mother more and brought a tint of tears that glazed her eyes. She tried to brush her eyes, but Anshik's sharp eyes noted it. He stepped on Kavya's legs.

"Ouch!"

"What?" she demanded.

"You told me you wanted to share your success story with your friend, right?"

"Huh?"

He stared at her. Rubbing her foot, she managed, "Yes."

She diverted Ananya's mind successfully.

"Happy that at least one of us could succeed," Ananya said, giving her a hug of happiness without a streak of jealousy.

"Hey, you talk as if you are going to work at Anshik's cafeteria all your life. You still have time, my girl. And who knows? Once you become a world-famous filmmaker, I will have to wait for my chance to get a role in your creations. Don't forget your long-time friend," she told her a little dramatically.

A regretful smile took over her lips, but she did not voice her denial. Arguments were not on the menu for the day.

"Hey, she did not say 'no'. This means you will get your role, Kavya," Anshik's father added jovially.

"And, Ananya, while we are on the topic, I love to act, and you have to give me a chance to play the hero in any of your stories," he pleaded teasingly, rubbing his big tummy.

Laughter took over Ananya, and she gave in after three long months.

"What are you laughing at? Am I not handsome like Anshik?" he pulled her legs.

Ananya gasped at his statement as her gaze met Anshik's. Dressed in a color combination like hers, he looked like his gorgeous self.

"Don't make her blush, Ankush," Sheela chided her husband.

"That is okay, aunty. I am happy to see you all as a family. But . . ." she stopped with a longing she could not hide.

"I miss my mom," she whimpered.

Sheela hugged her and brushed her eyes with her red cotton sari.

"Don't worry, *beti*. Your mother will always be with you," she blessed.

*****

The dinner switched to a silent mode post Ananya's confession. The siblings were reluctant to continue their funny banters in case their guest gets hurt.

Though Ananya had completed whatever was served, she did not know what she ate as she looked at her empty plate. Her depressed mind did not let her take part in the dinner wholeheartedly.

At times, she laughed, forgetting herself. But then she would feel guilty that she was selfish enough to laugh in a world without her mother. That thought wiped the little smile completely from her lips.

The clock displayed 8.30 p.m.

"I have to leave," she informed Kavya as her father joined them.

"Ananya."

"Yes, uncle," she responded politely.

"I would suggest that you stay here this weekend and relax. I know you went through a traumatizing period, and you definitely need a let-out."

"But . . ." she wanted to voice out her protest.

"You are like our daughter, Ananya. It would disturb us if we let you leave in this depressed state . . ."

She looked at the concern in his eyes.

"I know it is difficult overcoming your loss. But remember that time waits for no one. The world functions and does not care who is alive or who is dead."

"Uncle—"

"It is true, Ananya. Life is unfair sometimes. But we can't change the fact. Would your mother want you to stay this way, thinking about her and mourning for the rest of your life?"

She shook her head negatively.

"No one would want their dear ones to cry after their death. They want them to live and be happy. Your mother would wish the same for you."

He patted her head gently. Anshik stood as a silent spectator, watching them, and he nodded gratefully at his father.

"Time is a great healer, Ananya. I know you miss her a lot. But hold on to the wonderful memories you have of her. So that when you think of her, your lips will transform into a beautiful smile, recalling the special moments you had with her. That is the best homage we can give to the ones who have left us for eternity. Fate can take our loved ones away, but even destiny doesn't have the power to snatch their memories from us. It will stay with us forever for us to cherish."

Ananya's mind calmed a little, and she acknowledged with a nod as if she had no more to say.

"Good girl . . . not like my naughty darling daughter, Kavya," he appreciated, trying to loosen the atmosphere a little.

Kavya stuck her tongue out at her father but turned to her friend.

"Stay with us for this weekend, Ananya," said Ankush.

"You have been very kind, uncle and I don't want to take advantage of your kindness by troubling you," she informed with regret.

"Who said that this will trouble us?" Sheela queried and added, "I agree with Ankush. Stay with us."

Kavya cajoled, "Say yes, Anu."

Everyone had asked her to stay, but not Anshik. Was he considering her a burden to his family? She turned to him but was surprised to see his eyes asking her to stay.

"Alright, I'll stay. Thank you everyone for your concern. But I don't have any clothes," she exclaimed.

"Don't worry. I'll bring mine. I think we wear the same size and mine will fit you," volunteered Kavya.

After giving her the dresses, she showed the room next to hers.

"You can use this room, Ananya. If you need anything, wake up anyone from the family. We are all yours, right, Anshik?"

She dragged her brother into the conversation, who was about to go to his room, satisfied.

"What are you telling her?" he asked curiously.

"I said that we are all hers . . . I mean . . . she can consider each one of us as her family, right?" she winked.

"Yes, she can." He confirmed. She felt overwhelmed by his reply. At that moment, she felt loved with a loving family to take care of her, and she wanted to hold on to it.

"Good night, Ananya," they wished.

Ananya went into her room. It was beautiful, with green and yellow walls all around. Sleep eluded her despite the silky bed and the feathery pillows. A cool breeze greeted her as she stepped onto the balcony.

She walked along the balcony, holding the iron rail, and came out through the common balcony of the house at the end of the living room.

Anshik stood beside Ananya. He had heard the footsteps and had followed her. It surprised him to see her there.

"I thought you would have slept, Ananya," he told her from the back.

She jumped at his voice.

"What are you doing here?"

He raised his eyebrows at her absurd query.

"Yeah, I understand that this is your house. But I thought you would have already gone to bed."

"I heard some footsteps, and they brought me here."

"Oh, I am sorry, Anshik. I did not mean to disturb you." She shivered in the cold Pune weather.

Noticing the same, he removed his jerkins and passed it to her.

"Wear this; it will help."

"Don't you need it?"

"I am used to this cold weather, and I don't mind," declared Anshik.

Ananya wore his jerkins, though it was a couple of sizes too big for her. She could smell his perfume, and with it on, she felt secure, as if he had hugged her. Tugging the surrounding corners tightly, she reveled in the comfort it provided her.

Suddenly, she turned toward him. "Anshik, I understand what uncle said earlier, but still I need my mother back."

It shocked him as he took in her request. Seeing her eyes wet, he wiped her tears involuntarily, as if it was the most natural thing to do.

She wanted to bury her head inside his chest and stay there forever, taking in his support. But on what rights can she do that? She did not.

"The more I spend time with your family, the more I long for mine. I feel alone in this world," she murmured, eyes fixed on the night sky.

He put his fingers on her lips. "Never say that."

'*You have me* .' He wanted to assure her but could not.

"I know that no one can replace your mom. But you keep forgetting the rest of your family," he said while pulling her toward him.

She interrupted, "Father has already disowned me." There was an unspoken pain in her voice.

"You have your brother as well."

"Brother? He is my father's replica in all his thoughts."

Anshik continued, "And you have me."

"You?" For a moment, her heart fluttered at his assurance, and she looked at him anxiously.

"As a friend." Anshik vowed not to scare her with his emotions for now, since she had stated that he was her friend, even though he had reservations.

She felt disappointed with his words.

"Hah, a friend."

"That is what you want, right, Ananya?"

"Yes." She agreed.

He smiled at that. "Looks like you are unsure."

"No," she whispered as Anshik cupped her cheeks and searched for the truth in her eyes. She bent her head, avoiding his gaze.

With his fingers, he lifted her chin to read the denied truth.

Her red dupatta fluttered in the night sky with the breeze and restricted his vision. Patiently, he removed the obstruction away.

Her beautiful face was a sweet temptation. He gently bent and placed feathery kisses on her tears. "Never cry again, Ananya. I'll not let you," he commanded.

His words soothed her emotions and were quite therapeutic to her sadness. Slowly, she melted into his arms as if he were an addictive drug who could miraculously cure all her issues. That thought pushed her to hug him with all her might. They did not realize for how long they stood just like that.

He brushed the leftover tears off her cheeks. The slight touch made her shiver despite the warmth provided by his jerkins.

"Cold?" he enquired with concern.

She shook her head negatively, still in a daze.

He held her in his arms tightly and murmured, "Now you will feel better."

The moon was bright, and her face glittered despite the agony she was going through. With his fingers, he traced her lips and tugged the corners a little, feeling her softness.

"Smile, Ananya. Your lips should always stay this way."

She gave into her feelings and buried her head into his shoulders as she cried. She drew him closer, not realizing what she was doing or how close they were, and muttered against his lips emotionally, "Please stay with me. I need you, Anshik . . ."

Her emotional wall cracked, though she tried hard to make it stay intact. Anshik was not made of stone. Her words touched the chords of his heart.

"I'll always be with you, Anu."

She was surprised to see tears in his eyes, as if he had missed her terribly all these years. He tightened their hug as if he would never let her go.

"You are lying," she criticized, letting out her pain with her emotional tirade.

"No, Anu."

Snapping his hands, she held his collar again and demanded, "Then, why did you leave me all those years ago?

"How dare you leave me?" she cried.

He stood silently, taking all her blows without a sound. She vented out her anger on him, yet he did not retaliate.

Pushing him away, she demanded, "You don't have an answer, do you?"

On that note, she stormed out from the balcony, leaving him to his dear solitude, not noticing that he had also gone through the same emotional trauma as her during their breakup.

"Anu . . ." He turned away from her because he didn't want to show her how emotionally damaged she had made him. A few tears spontaneously spilled onto his hands, despite his best efforts to remain composed.

CHAPTER 9

The Past Catches Up

Instead of raking through the aching memories from our past, why don't we create lovely, unforgettable ones along the way that we could cherish forever till eternity?

Anshik closed his bedroom with regret. He could not blame her for the lack of faith she had in him, since he couldn't explain why he left her years ago. No relationship in this world could survive without trust. Desperation took him over as he thumped his bed.

He wanted her to believe in him again, and he knew it would be tough to earn her love this time. His heart instructed him to give them some time to rebuild the trust that had persisted between them before.

"I'll bring back the strong connection we had, Ananya," he vowed.

His present intentions were the only thing he wanted her to concentrate on, rather than the sadness of the past. He did not want her to forget the past completely, because not all the memories they had created were miserable. In fact, except for their last meeting, everything had been perfect.

To him, certain memories from their past were nostalgic, and he ached to relive them again. With a longing he could not control, he went to open the drawer inside his wardrobe and took out a gray box.

Placing it on his bed, he sat by its side, fingering the delicate patterns of the wood. The box was painted gray, but the memories inside were anything but gray. All the colors of his life were locked inside.

After three long years, he unlocked the box with fingers that trembled a little, thinking of what he had lost. He peered through the contents and knew that the Pandora of memories he had unlocked had the power to disturb and distract him. But a secret part of him yearned to reminisce about those golden days. It was the treasure trove of his life, and on any day, he would trade all his money for the same.

There were insignificant items—her hair clip, a broken stud, a pen, which she had gifted him. They would hold no meaning to an outsider, but to him they told stories of their precious past. Underneath them was the card, which had changed his life.

It was handmade and simply said—"Start living again"

He set the card aside. He took the dust-bound diary, filled with regret for what could have been. Their beautiful story was documented by him. Although he enjoyed writing, he stopped when she left.

'Does she wield that kind of power in my life? Come on, don't kid yourself. You know you would do anything for her.'

Dusting the front flap, he opened the diary and dove into the past, which brought them together three years ago.

*****

Three years ago

Place: *Pune*

Ananya Mehta stepped into her friend Kavya Dhawan's apartment. Each family member had their own key, so they didn't disturb one another. Ananya knew that Kavya's mother—Sheela—worked as a primary school teacher in a nearby school. Kavya had revealed to her that she had a brother named Anshik, who had completed his engineering and was looking for a job. They had lived royally and were well-off until the worst had befallen their family. Kavya's father, Ankush Dhawan, had become bedridden after an accident that damaged his spine.

As an experienced electrical engineer, he headed the innovation department in a corporate company that sold microchips. They had lived in a palatial home prior to his accident. After his fall, the company threw him out with no consideration, leaving Kavya's mother alone to cope with the financial pressure.

To top it all, they had demanded money from his family as compensation, as Ankush's car had his latest finding—the primary chip that could have yielded them crores if it had not been broken in the accident. They had also filed a case against them, persisting that the only version of the chip was gone, which the family strongly doubted, but they could not prove it.

They had to sell their bigger house to pay the money and move into their first home, which was smaller, yet it was Ankush Dhawan's special and sentimental property, as he had purchased it at the beginning of his career. Their father had often stated that after moving to this home, he had become highly successful, and it was a lucky charm for them all.

Kavya had also told her that her mother kept pushing her brother to pitch in with some financial help to support the family and arrange money for their father's operation, so that he could walk again.

But the problem was that he could not clear the job interviews that came his way, which constantly became a heated source of argument between the mother and the son.

Though it was a simple two-bedroom apartment, the home decor was elegant and beautiful. The living room walls were yellow, and the kitchen was cozy. The furniture, though wooden, was modern and space-saving to fit into their cramped space. With the fresh smell of *paratha* taunting her nostrils, the place felt like home to the younger Ananya.

In a simple white T-shirt and blue jeans, Kavya waited patiently for her friend's comments on her home. This was the first time she had brought home a friend.

"What is the verdict?"

"Wow, it is beautiful, Kavya," she enthused.

Sheela Dhawan came out of the kitchen and hugged Ananya.

"Aunty, you are getting your beautiful cotton sari crushed," she warned.

"I don't mind. I have to thank you, my dear, for helping my daughter from those bullies. Ever since that day, Kavya had been chanting your name and wanted to bring you home. For a college girl, you are brave," she appreciated her.

"That is okay, aunty. I just pushed Kavya to stand for herself, but in the end, it was her brother who helped her," she replied modestly.

"I know my son helped as well. But where is he?" She turned to Kavya.

"*Bhaiya* told me that he will be back soon, ma. He has gone out to get some snacks for us."

Ananya was curious to meet Anshik. She had spoken to him only once with his helmet on, and this was the first time she was going to see him. She thought about how her friendship with Kavya had strengthened over the past couple of weeks. Into the final year of their college, Ananya and Kavya did an English Literature course, and they were friends even prior to that incident.

Kavya was abnormally silent for a week, which pushed Ananya to demand an answer from her. She had confided that she was being stalked by a group of ruffians daily on her way to college. The head of the group, Raghav, had a crush on Kavya and forced her to go out with him.

Though she had denied him decently, he stalked her daily and kept pestering her to date him. Kavya was scared and did not know how to handle them. But she had confided to Ananya that she wanted to tackle them independently, as her family already had enough troubles on their plate, managing their bedridden father.

"The more you show them you are frightened, they will take advantage of your fear, Kavya," Ananya had advised.

"If you don't want to inform your family, then you should be bold."

"This is all new to me, Ananya," Kavya wailed.

"As if I am dealing with this all day," Ananya retorted.

That is when a spark of an idea hit her.

"Why don't you come with me and give that rowdy a piece of your mind? You are strong enough to deal with him. To be honest, Ananya, I don't have a daring personality like yours. And I am scared just by looking at Raghav."

Giving in to her pleading eyes, Ananya confirmed, "Alright, I will. But you will not always have an *Ananya* around you. You need to know how to save yourself, given any scenario. Got it?"

Kavya nodded. She knew she had to be equipped and better prepared for the future.

The next day, as per their plan, Ananya walked with Kavya to the bus stop.

"That is him—Raghav," Kavya pointed.

Ananya turned to see a dark, lean, muscular guy, whose height was a little more than hers. The odd thing about his face was an overgrown mustache. His lengthy hair touched his shoulders, giving him a villainous look. He was talking with a group of his friends, who were all unkempt, with ripped shirts and pants.

The moment he saw Kavya, Raghav ignored the rest of his friends and walked toward her. Kavya's mobile rang. She took it out urgently to see that her brother, Anshik, was calling her.

"How dare someone call you?" scolded Raghav.

"That is my brother," Kavya murmured.

"That is okay then," he concluded, tugging the mobile from her and disconnecting the call.

"So who have you brought with you? She is also beautiful . . ."

"Don't you think so?" He turned to his gang.

Many boys in the group lifted their hands.

He laughed. "You have several fans here. But my eyes see only my darling, Kavya," he commented wryly.

"How dare you?" Ananya came forward.

"This flower shouts!" he told them in astonishment.

"You are an indecent boy who does not know how to behave with girls," she declared.

"Don't take that tone with me, girl."

"Look around you. We are standing at a public bus stand. What can you do to us?"

"Ha ha. Do you see someone coming to help you?"

As Ananya turned to others, they averted their eyes as if they did not want to get into trouble.

"That is my power. The inspector is my close friend." He laughed, revealing his connection with the higher-ups.

"Is it?" Ananya was sure that Raghav would be forced to take a step back if someone spoke to him in public. But that was not working out. She quickly thought of a plan B.

That is when her eyes caught the mobile he had snatched from Kavya. Instead of disconnecting the call, he had switched it on. Kavya's brother was on the other end, listening to the entire conversation.

"Don't underestimate the power of the public, Raghav. You can't harm a hair on our head when we are standing exactly at the Shaniwar Wada bus stop."

Ananya had absolutely no idea what kind of guy Anshik was. But all she knew was no brother would sit at the other end after hearing someone teasing his sister. She tried to stall Raghav, dragging the conversation, and provoked him to retaliate verbally before he could exhibit his physical strength. Minutes passed by as the scenario worsened.

"Give her mobile back." She went close and pulled it out

of his hold, hoping that he wouldn't notice that someone was on the other side of the call.

She passed it to Kavya, with the backside visible to all.

"How dare you take that from my hand?" screamed Raghav.

Knowing that Ananya was a stronger opponent, he turned to Kavya and demanded, "Are you a fool, Kavya. Don't you know what I would do if you defied me—your future husband?"

He raised his hand.

"Don't you dare . . ."

Ananya interrupted him and clasped his hands. With her other hand, she slapped him hard on his cheeks.

That was the first time Anshik saw Ananya. To him, she looked like an avenging angel. He had no time to remove his helmet as he drove his bike toward the epicenter of the unfolding drama.

"Kavya," he shouted.

"*Bhaiya*!" She turned in surprise.

Getting off the bike, he dwarfed Raghav and his gang.

"You leave, sis."

"But. . ."

"I said leave."

Gripping Raghav's hands, he threw him out of their reach.

Noting Ananya had not left, he held her and pushed her aside. "You go ahead with Kavya. You are Ananya, right? I will take care of them."

She could sense his intent but did not want to leave him alone.

"But, I want to help. I can't leave you alone," she was determined.

For a moment, her reply surprised him. "The police will be here any moment. You leave. Take Kavya with you," he reiterated.

There was an aura of toughness around him. She nodded.

*****

Mrs. Sheela Dhawan and her daughter cooked dinner while Ananya stayed in the living room. Having returned with the coffee tray, Kavya noticed that Ananya was present physically, but her mind was elsewhere.

"Where are you, Ananya?" Kavya snapped her fingers before her face.

Coming to her senses, she spoke without thinking.

"I was thinking about the horrifying incident that happened last week. Your brother was smart enough to understand my clues Kavya, and came to help you like a hero."

Anshik walked in at Ananya's last statement.

Kavya turned to see her brother inside and giggled. "Meet the hero then, Ananya, my brother, Anshik Dhawan."

"And, *bhaiya*, meet my best friend who stood beside me during trouble, Miss Ananya Mehta."

"Glad to meet you, Ananya. I just did what any brother would do." He extended his hands, genuinely pleased to meet her.

Wearing a greenish-blue cotton dress, she was charming and appeared innocent. The arches in her eyebrows highlighted the structure of her attractive face. Her shoulder-length hair was loose, and she had a small black *bindi* on her forehead. She looked modern without losing the traditional touch. He remembered how she had slapped that ruffian boldly, without an afterthought. Beauty with boldness was a rare trait, and this girl had everything.

Anshik's mind memorized her image within a second. Such was her impact on him.

The moment their eyes met, an invisible chord connected them.

He was casually dressed in his green T-shirt and jeans, yet he appeared powerful to her. His tall stature and clean-shaven face captivated her. His hair was swept back, and she could see that his angular face with a broad forehead gave him a rugged appearance. But the way he had stood for his sister created an instant liking for him, showing her that underneath the tough exterior he projected, there was a caring person.

She looked at him as if she was in a daze.

"Ananya," he called her, bringing her back to the world of reality as she blushed at her thoughts.

She accepted his handshake, marking the beginning of a meaningful relationship between them. Even then, he had known that he would never forget this moment all his life.

"Come on . . . this little sister of mine wanted me to get some *pav-bhaji* for you from Ram *bhaiya's* shop at the corner. Try them," he said.

Ananya nodded happily and joined them.

The *pav-bhaji* triggered a lovely bond between her and the siblings. Anshik, being the elder one, took care of them both. She met them during the weekends, and he took both girls to the nearby coffee shop, where they talked about everything under the sun.

The friendly rapport between Anshik and Ananya grew stronger each day, just like her bonding with Kavya. With a broader mindset, Sheela Dhawan thought little about the trio going out together. She wanted someone like Ananya to steer Kavya in the right direction.

After a couple of weeks, Ananya told her friend that she wanted to meet her father. "I don't want to pry, though." She added.

"What is there to pry?" Kavya took Ananya to her father's room.

He was on his bed, trying to hold a book steady with his right hand, but his mission failed, and he dropped the object on his head.

"Oh God . . ." Ananya ran to him as they stepped in.

"No, it is alright. I can use my left hand. Only my right leg and hand don't cooperate with me," he told her apologetically. But his eyes looked inquiringly at the newcomer.

"Papa, this is Ananya, my best friend."

Ananya smiled at him warmly, and Anshik joined them.

"Not only mine. *Bhaiya's* best friend as well," she confided to her dad.

"Oh, is it?" her dad turned curiously to her.

"I don't know, uncle. Ask your son."

"Hmm, what do you say, Ansh?"

He ignored his father's query. He knew his father was trying to turn the attention elsewhere. His papa's pathetic effort to hold the book with his right hand disturbed him. He was making no improvement.

"All I say is I want to see you up and running, papa."

The father tugged his son's chin affectionately.

"And I know that time will come soon."

"Yes, papa, can't wait for that." Kavya kissed her dad's cheeks.

The friendly bond that they shared with their father touched Ananya. Her relationship with her father had always been rocky from her childhood.

The moment they came out, Sheela halted Anshik.

"What happened at the interview yesterday?"

He averted his eyes from his mother's prying ones.

"Flopped?" she prompted him.

"I cleared the technical round, ma. But the HR round did not go as planned," he told her regretfully.

"You might have exhibited your arrogance as usual," she criticized.

"No, I just spoke the truth instead of sugar coating my words."

"And to that, they would have retaliated, saying that you are a guy with too much of an attitude," his mother criticized.

Ananya turned in surprise. It was as if she had seen that interview in person.

"Don't look surprised, Ananya. The same has been happening since he completed his engineering. He says that he would only go to a job if the nature of the job and the people are to his liking."

"What is wrong with that, aunty?" she argued, supporting Anshik.

"Nothing. But we are in a financial crunch, Ananya. He needs to go out. Earn and bring money for his father's operation."

The moment she spoke about Ankush, her voice wobbled emotionally.

"The operation is getting delayed with our financial issues. My teacher's salary is just enough to run the family. How could we save for his operation then?"

"Ma, please," Anshik squatted beside her.

"No, you don't understand the seriousness, Anshik." She pushed his hands.

"Ma, how could I do something which I don't like or work with people whom I don't like?"

"Why don't you understand and be responsible once? It has been two years, and you still have not found a job. The first year, I let you explore and play a little. But this year, with your father's accident, things have changed. We have no other choice. Get yourself a job, and if it is not to your liking, you need to accept it for the sake of your father. Did you not note the excitement in his eyes when you spoke about him walking again?"

Anshik turned to the other side with fisted arms in anger.

"And there is a beautiful quality in life—we term it as 'sacrifice'. I think you need to learn it for the sake of people you love," she persisted, ending on a stern note.

The pressure to find himself a job mounted on him and disturbed the equilibrium in his life. He stormed out in hopelessness, without saying a word to his mother. "Keep running away from the truth, Anshik," Sheela screamed behind his back.

"Ma, calm down." Kavya stopped her.

"You know him. He is not technically weak. In fact, *bhaiya* is better than all his friends working at corporate companies. You know his strength well, ma. But his strength has become his weakness now. He is overqualified for these types of jobs, and the interviewers are not intelligent enough to hold a person of his caliber."

"I don't care, Kavya. I know he is extremely talented and waiting for the right role. But we have little time. He must

101

give in a little and take up whatever comes his way. Papa is his responsibility now."

"Ma, *bhaiya* is not the one who shuns his responsibilities," she argued.

"Ask him to prove it then," Sheela slammed.

Kavya signaled to Ananya. "I'll handle ma. Take care of *bhaiya*," she whispered into her ears.

She ran to Anshik, feeling sad for him.

CHAPTER 10

Anshik's Life Map

Be your own cartographer and make out your life map with all potentially feasible routes that could take you toward happiness.

"Anshik, please wait!" shouted Ananya as he took the key and was about to drive off. He did not stop, not even at her pleading voice.

She ran behind him as he took his seat.

"No, you can't."

With those words, she climbed onto the backside of his bike.

"What are you doing, Ananya? Please go," he chided.

She ignored his anger.

"I'll not. I will not leave you alone when you are angry, Ansh."

"Then it is your choice. Don't blame me," he told her sternly and raised the accelerator on his bike.

She fell on his back with an abrupt jerk. "Oh God!"

But there was no stopping him. He drove madly, breaking all the speed limits, twisting and twirling his bike as if he was on fire.

'Mahadev, please keep us safe and I don't want any trouble from the traffic police,' she prayed.

There was not even the slightest drip in his speed, even when they crossed the speed breakers. She gripped the iron bars at the side firmly, tackling her bumpiest ride ever. But she was losing her hold and was sure that she would fall off with the next bump.

Realizing that he was entirely out of his mind, she closed her eyes, clasped his back tight, and rested her head on him. After a crazy ride, he switched off his bike.

She opened her eyes and observed where he had stopped. He waited for her to get down. Her hug seemed to have appeased him somehow, and he asked, "Are you alright?"

She nodded as he dragged her to him.

"Silly girl. Why did you risk yourself joining me?"

She pushed him back. "I could ask you the same question. What caused you to drive like a maniac? You put yourself at risk too."

Her heart was still in her mouth.

"I needed to clear my thoughts," he told her gruffly.

"How? By killing yourself and others?" she demanded aggressively.

He did not reply. "Turn your aggression toward something productive," she told him. Silence prevailed. Ananya's voice came down.

"Never do this again, Ansh," she whispered, looking into his eyes, and continued, "I was scared."

"I warned you," he retaliated.

"I was scared . . . not for me, but for you."

He looked deep into her eyes and read her sincerity. That forced him to drop his veil of anger, which had assisted him in covering his hurt earlier.

"You can never understand what I am going through, Ananya."

"How do you know?"

He gave a sigh.

"I don't know how, but the moment you feel something, I can feel it too," she confessed.

Anshik stopped at her words. "What did you say?

She pushed him forward, ignoring his question.

"Nothing important, Ansh. But where are we?" she questioned him as she noted her surroundings.

"This is the Broken Trishul temple."

"Broken Trishul?"

"It got its name because the trishul in Lord Shiva's hands is broken. Built years ago, no one took the responsibility to repair this temple. Many people don't come here because the trishul is broken. Not even the priest comes here regularly to do poojas. But I come here on days when I need some peace of mind or to get answers to the problems that haunt my mind."

Except for one or two people here and there, the place was deserted. But as Anshik said, the temple was serene and calmed her, bringing out an unexplainable peace between them.

"You are right. This is indeed a wonderful place. I feel like I could meditate here forever."

Turning to him, she demanded, "Now tell me, why did you rush off like that?"

He walked toward the side bench carved out of stone. Positioned perfectly under the shade of an enormous mango tree, Anshik and Ananya sat on it.

"I am going through a phase gone through by all the unemployed youth throughout our country."

She did not deny it.

With a sigh, he continued, "The family pressure mounts on us, Ananya, before we figure out what we want. Situations vary for each one of us, but the moment we are out of the college, they expect us to work from day one, bringing in revenue for the family."

Ananya gave him space to vent his feelings.

"Not that I don't want to work or be responsible. But I found nothing to my liking. How can I stay in a place with no genuine interest? I cannot fake it. But my father is waiting for the day when he can walk again. And we need the money to get him operated on."

His anger against the unfairness of life threatened to come out, and his hand hit the side of the stone bench in frustration.

Ananya was sure it hurt like hell, yet he did not flinch.

Taking in what he said, Ananya took his hands and cradled them. Affectionately, she fingered his dented hand and murmured, "And your mother is angry at you. She wants you to pick up the first job that comes your way."

"I don't blame her. Earlier, she was supportive of my feelings. But she changed with my father's accident. The worst part is, I know that she is right, and I am just angry with myself. I am making my father suffer because I can't tolerate a job that I don't care for."

She kept brushing the redness in his hands. The pain subsided a little.

Despite his rudeness, she kept caring for him. That moved him, yet he did not show that.

"Why don't you find something you like then?"

"Not that easy, Ananya. And you don't know how difficult it is to find a job that you love."

"It might be hard. But tell me from your perspective. Why aren't you getting job offers?"

"My attitude. That is what they tell me."

"I agree." She laughed.

His lips curved.

"Finally, I have made you laugh, Ansh."

He nodded endearingly and his eyes shone with tenderness at the way she was still holding his wounded hand.

"I'll not term you as a person with a harsh attitude. You just say what you feel. So let me prepare a list of the skills at which you are good. Technical skills—check. Frank—check. Communication—check. And I remember the manner you managed Kavya's bullies. And your sister told me . . . you made them listen to you and changed them for good."

Her list sounded impressive to his ears.

"Oh God, why did no one notice this?"

"You are a born leader, Ansh. You are not meant to work under someone. Why don't you start a venture where you are your own boss?"

Her words pulled him out of the rut he was presently stuck in. It made sense, and why did he not realize this earlier? Ananya had to point that out.

The anger within him dissipated as he noted the angel who had chased him to calm him down. Her face was bare of makeup, but at twenty-one, she looked stunning in her ethnic black salwar and a red dupatta. She had her hair tied into a bouncy, high ponytail. Anshik felt hard to avert his gaze from her. His anger gave way to an unnamed feeling, and she was still holding his hand. His heartbeat went up by a notch, which he tried his best to ignore.

"What do you say?" she prompted him with enthusiasm in her world.

He acknowledged her with a slight nod.

"I agree and I regret not thinking about this earlier."

"Oh then, that is great. We have a solution now." She let go of his hand and revealed her enthusiasm by rewarding him with a hug and a kiss on his cheek.

"Happy for you, Ansh," she crooned in his ears.

Anshik was stunned. Her actions fueled his accelerating heart.

'Control yourself, Anshik . . .'

"Ananya," he called out.

Realizing that she was still holding him in her circle of arms, she blushed as she let go of him.

"Sorry, I got carried away. But I see a CEO in the making. Let bygones be bygones. Think that tomorrow is day one of your new life."

She took a notepad and wrote the words.

"Start living again.

Best wishes,

Ananya."

She pushed the note into his hands. "Ansh, as you said, many people go through this horrific period of unemployment. All they need to find is the right path for them. It might take some time, but with passing years, they will definitely reach there."

"Hmm, how does such *gyan* and philosophy come out of a little girl?"

"Little? I am in my final year of college." She put her hands on her hips.

"Are you not?" He wanted her to reaffirm.

If she confessed that she had grown up, he wondered how he would convince his heart any further not to kiss her. Because that was the only reason, he kept telling himself to control his wayward feelings toward her.

"Ansh, I am a devil in disguise, sent by God to torture you." She laughed.

He laughed wholeheartedly. "The devil will not run behind me, trying to sort out my problems."

"Devil or not. I have to be strong enough. Because my life is not that simple, as you see."

He lifted his eyebrows, prompting her to continue. This was the first time she opened up to him, and he wanted to know every bit about her.

"Though I am in my final year, completing my graduation is an uphill task for me."

"Why?"

"I come from an orthodox society and a family where a woman's sole purpose of life is to get married. My father is an accountant working for a landlord, who owns five farms at Shivapur."

"Yeah. I know Shivapur . . . a beautiful, greenish area," added Anshik.

"Shivapur is beautiful," she agreed and continued, "Papa's end goal for me is marriage. And spending money on my education is a sin for him with his meager income."

There was an odd inflection in her voice.

"But he does not mind spending it on my brother's education, though. To him, that is an investment. *Bhaiya* is pursuing his higher studies at present. He wants him to become a part of a big corporate organization, so that he can walk proudly in his village. He has confidence that my brother will be there for him in his old age. I can do that as well. But he does not care."

Anshik watched her keenly as multiple emotions flitted across her face, but one dominated throughout—pain.

"All he plans for me is my wedding, as if I was born just for that. That is the best I can do in my life to keep him proud and happy. To him, the chance to complete my graduation is an additional bonus that he has given. I think I have been allowed to complete it, just because he can print the degree against my name on the wedding cards and not on my resume."

"Are you not interested in marriage?"

"Oh, come on, Ansh. I am." She paused, giving him an approving look.

"But not right now, though. I have my own plans for my life," she completed.

"What is your plan?" he asked, ruffling her hair.

"I want to create stories."

Noting his confusion, she elaborated, "I want to be a filmmaker someday—make movies on the big screen or the television that connect with the audience. I want to entertain them and help them learn the lessons of life."

"I am surprised, Ananya. You have a different yet a beautiful dream."

"Thanks, Ansh." She held his hand with affection.

"And do you know what will happen if I tell my papa that I want to create stories and be a filmmaker in the future?"

Anshik nodded negatively.

"He would throw me out of the house."

"Really?"

"Yes, sometimes I regret being born as a girl in this society."

He put his finger on her lips.

"Never say that again. You don't know how blessed you are."

"I am going through these hiccups just because I am a girl. Don't I have the right to choose my career and live the life I desire?"

"I agree. Then fight for it. Don't give into their unreasonable demands. Honor your needs, and not those of the society."

"Hope everything works out as you say, Ansh."

"It will," he promised.

"I have to hug and kiss you now," he threatened.

"Why?"

"When I agreed to your solution, you kissed me and now it is my turn."

He came closer to her, and Ananya pushed him back playfully.

Ignoring that, he tugged her, and she was caught in his hold. Blowing her hair gently away, he admitted, "Do you know what is best about you? Your fighting spirit and loyalty."

"Really? Don't flatter me, Ansh."

"Why would I?"

"So that you could kiss me."

She tried to get out of his firm hold, but he would not let her leave.

"I don't need a reason to kiss you Ananya."

She blushed at his words.

"I will kiss you when I am sure that you will respond . . ."

His statement took the breath out of her lungs, and she stood captivated, like a dove caught in the hunter's snare.

"And I feel you would not deny me this second . . ."

With those words, Anshik kissed Ananya on her cheeks. A peculiar new sensation shot through her at his touch. She was lost as his hands slid down and held her tightly. Her heart thumped madly at his closeness. She could feel his breath on her neck with his head bent a little. A sinking sensation in her stomach conquered her, and she lost her balance, and he tightened his hold.

He stepped back to look into her eyes.

"Thank you, Anu. You don't know what difference you have made in my life today, and I will never forget that. Tumbling in different directions, I was confused. My path is set and I'll focus."

He continued, "You are a step ahead of me. You already know what you want. Go behind your dreams, Ananya. Don't give in to emotional blackmail, even to people who are close to you."

She nodded in agreement. He opened the ruffled paper she had given him earlier. "START LIVING AGAIN."

They read the line together.

"Let the bygones be bygones . . . let us start afresh," she enthused.

At her age, everything was black or white. And to Ananya, everything was white at present in her state.

He brushed his lips against her forehead, unable to let her go. She closed her eyes gently, enveloped with a sense of security. She was in the safest haven, and she believed he would let nothing bad happen to her.

CHAPTER 11

First Love

When you are near, my heart skips a beat.
Though I cribbed about the garbage on the streets
till yesterday, today my attention is on the delicate
pink flowers. I smile at everyone and laugh at their
silly jokes. How do I name this unnamed, crazy
feeling that has taken over me?

Since their visit to the Broken Trishul temple, their relationship stabilized and became stronger. They could sense the indiscernible connection between their souls. Ananya's heart secretly desired to see him, and she visited Kavya's house frequently, hoping to get a glance of him, satisfying the craving in her heart.

The allure he eluded tugged her toward him, and she could not stay away. As soon as she saw a chance to connect with him remotely without seeming too obvious, she took it. She could not explain to herself why she felt this way.

It was Friday evening. The last bell went off.

"We have not completed the script," warned Kavya.

They had their drama competition on Monday, and the script was not ready yet. They had to practice as well. With their exams this week, they could not do it.

"Come to my home, Ananya. Let us complete our task today."

"I promised my mother that I'll help her today in preparing the snacks," Ananya replied with regret.

"Please, Anu, we need your help."

Akshay and Raghu joined Kavya. "Yes, we do. Our team must win. I have never seen a better script writer than you."

"Keep your flattery to yourself, Akshay. I want to help you. But I have promised ma and if I am late, my dad will ask too many questions. It would become tough to manage him."

"Let aunty do it then. You don't worry," suggested Kavya.

Unable to deny her friend's request, and with the thought of meeting Anshik, she agreed. She looked at her watch. It was 4.00 p.m. She messaged her mother, informing her she might be late, as she had her drama practice.

"Please handle papa." She added a voice note.

"That should do the trick," commented Kavya.

Together, they took an auto and reached Kavya's house.

Anshik answered the door. He was working on an initial plan for his start-up. Surprised to see Ananya at the door, he smiled. The moment he saw her, a feeling of exhilaration took him over as if he had had a couple of drinks. In a yellow kurti and red leggings, she appeared slender. A slight tint of lip-gloss added a subtle shade of pink to her luscious lips.

Golden hoops adorned her ears, and she wore a pair of fancy black slippers. Anshik took all this in a single glance. The mere sight of her caused his insides to flip.

Making his face bland, he wished, "Hello, girls . . ."

But his smile turned to a frown as he noted the other boys in the group.

Kavya made the introduction.

"*Bhaiya*, this is Akshay and Raghu from my class. We are doing a skit this Monday. Ananya is the script writer and the heroine of our play. They have come here for practice."

"Alright. Who is the hero?" he asked them curiously.

"Me," declared Raghu. "The handsome guy in the group," he proclaimed.

"How modest." Kavya laughed. But her brother's face became serious.

The moment they went inside Kavya's room, Anshik became restless. His mind pictured Ananya and Raghu practicing together, and that vision taunted him. He shook his head to clear his mind and tried to continue his work, pushing aside his unwanted thoughts, but he could not. Fifteen unproductive minutes went by.

With a sigh, he switched off his laptop. Anyway, he was done. The door to the room was partly open. He saw that they had started their practice.

Kavya teased Ananya, who played Shivi.

"Has my Shivi fallen hard and given her heart to someone else?" Shivi nodded her head, blushing.

"How does he look?

"Tall, olive complexioned—"

"Wah, he sounds as if he has dropped right out of a romantic novel."

"I agree. He looks like a Greek God with all his wavy black hair."

"Oh God, Shivi. I am happy for you. The bug of love has bitten you. You could not evade this bite either."

She swirled her around. "What is his name?"

"Ansh . . ." She stopped at the right moment. "Anshrech."

The guys cheered. "Perfect, girls. But, Ananya, Raghu's name in the skit is Manav. You got the name wrong. Correct it next time. Let us rehearse the next scene . . ."

Ananya nodded sheepishly. She almost gave herself up with that mistake. Glad that no one figured that out. The others enacted the next scene, and she joined Raghu, her love in the drama.

Raghu pulled Ananya close and murmured, "I love you, Shivi . . . and I am sure you love me too."

Observing them from the entrance, Anshik's hands itched to throw Raghu out of his house. *'How dare he touch my girl?'*

'Stop it, Raghu.' His mind kept murmuring, unable to bear his touch on Ananya.

'But when did Ananya become mine?'

'She was always yours,' his mind told him with clarity.

Shaking away those disturbing thoughts, his attention went back to the couple who were practicing.

"Prove it." Shivi put her hand on his shoulders.

"I can do it by kissing you."

Enough was enough. He could not control the jealous monster that peeped out, with no regard for anyone else.

He barged inside noisily as they stopped the rehearsal. Picking up the script, his eyes ran through the scene they enacted.

"This is absurd."

"What is?" demanded Ananya, observing him from head to toe. This gave her a perfect chance to do that without being too open.

His casual red shirt and blue jeans fit his muscular frame to perfection and added to his height. Physically fit, his hair was messed up at the front, as if he ran his hands through them. With his commanding and masculine stance, she could pick up the angry vibes from him.

Not answering her, he turned to Raghu.

"Why should you kiss Ananya here?"

"Correction, it is Manav kissing Shivi, not Raghu kissing Ananya. Anyway, it is a part of the script," argued Raghu.

"I think these scenes are not required," Anshik retorted.

"We are doing a final year college script for God's sake, and we are twenty, not ten."

"*Bhaiya*, please. This scene will show the strength of their love," his sister pleaded.

"A kiss is definitely not required to prove the love between the characters," he spoke out.

"It was just going to be a peck on her cheek," reasoned Kavya.

"No, take that scene out. It is not required." Anshik was adamant. Kavya had never seen her brother acting in this peculiar way. He had not even intruded once with any of their earlier friends' catch-up. What was wrong with him? Looking at his obstinacy, this was not the right time to argue with him over a harmless scene.

Ananya, who was silently watching, joined their conversation.

"Ansh, calm down."

"Guys, Kavya's brother is right. This scene is not required."

"But you were the one who included that in the first place," argued Raghu.

"I think we can show the intensity of their love through some other way. Let me rewrite that scene."

She took the paper back and changed the scene. Losing interest in Ananya's writing, the other three discussed the climax, leaving Anshik all alone.

He sat next to Ananya, and she turned to him with a query. "Are you alright?"

"No, until you show me the scene you have rewritten."

"Why is that so important to you?"

The people in the room were forgotten as they were absorbed in their own world.

"Don't you know?" he queried back, holding her gaze.

She blinked her innocent eyes. "No."

"Have you rewritten the scene?"

Kavya broke the moment. Taking a quick glance at what she had written, Anshik informed them, "This should be fine."

*****

Months went by. Ananya and Kavya were in their last semester, and Anshik had completed his plan for his company. He had found a few investors who were ready to invest in his start-up, but he still needed an additional loan of 20 lakh to complete the setup.

He met several friends to arrange the amount, which was not happening. After a fruitless trip to chase a lead for the loan amount, Anshik returned home at seven in the evening. Garlands hung at the side of the front entrance, and he was astonished.

Upon entering, he saw that the house was decorated with flowers. Kavya rushed to his side. They were joined by Ananya. Dressed in *ghagras*, they both looked stunning, but Ananya looked divine to him. His mother wore a green silk sari with interleaved yellow threads.

"What is special today, ma?"

"Today is Raksha Bandhan, *bhaiya* and you left early in the morning. I could not tie you Rakhi, and I was waiting for you the entire day," she pouted, revealing her mock anger.

"Am sorry, Kavya . . . with all the tension around the loan for my start-up, I completely forgot," he apologized.

She hugged him. "I know, bro. Hence, I don't have a complaint. What is the big deal, anyway? Let us celebrate. ma said that we have got an hour of good muhurta left till 7.30 p.m."

Mrs. Sheela Dhawan went in to bring the items out for the pooja. "Come on, Kavya, help me."

Anshik and Ananya were left alone. She looked pretty in her red satin top and an ivory-colored silk skirt. Her ankles were adorned with silver anklets, and her hands jingled with the sound of the red glass bangles. She wore red lipstick and had smeared some eyeliner. With a traditional bindi on her forehead and braided hair, she knew she looked nice.

"You look stunning, Anu," he appreciated her.

She blushed at his compliment.

"One look at you and all my troubles melt," he confessed involuntarily.

"You look good too, wearing your formal attire," she returned his compliment.

She looked at his full-sleeved purple shirt and ivory pants.

"Are you kidding me? I roamed around in this outfit the entire day on the dusty roads of Pune," he remarked wryly.

"That adds to the charm."

"You are enough to boost my confidence any day." He chuckled.

"What are your guys laughing about?" asked Kavya, cutting their laughter.

"Nothing important, sis. Let us begin the rituals," he distracted his sister.

"Not before you change your clothes." His mother gave him a new set.

"Change and come back soon. We will wait for you."

He quickly changed into a sleeveless white-and-black hooded T-shirt and casual black pants, looking incredible.

The moment he stepped out, Kavya commented, "Yeah, you were right, Ananya. This suits him."

"You chose it for me?" he probed.

"Yes." Before he could ask anything further, she prompted Kavya, "Time to begin your rituals. It is almost 7.30 p.m."

Kavya performed the *aarti* with all the love of a sister and applied *tilak* on his forehead. She fed him a piece of chocolate, and Anshik did the same. Kavya then tied a handmade piece of Rakhi on his hands. The mother observed the siblings, giving out a happy sigh.

Turning to her, Kavya requested, "Ma, could you please bring dinner to the table?"

"I will," she agreed and went in, wiping away the tears of joy from her eyes.

Kavya duly noted the longing in Ananya's eyes.

"Are you missing your brother?" she demanded.

"Yes, I am. He is in the UK for his higher studies."

"So if you require a temporary brother to fill in his shoes, why don't you do the honors to Ansh *bhaiya*?"

Ananya gasped. Kavya was playing at what? She was sure that she had already suspected something was going on between them, though she had never confessed her feelings to her friend.

Looking at her comical reaction, Anshik pushed her. "Yes, why don't you?"

"He is your brother, Kavya. Not mine," she told them clear-cut.

"Ananya is right. She is not my sister and never could be. Most of all, I don't need her as my sister, when I have you."

His dramatic declaration did not fool Kavya.

"Instead of flattering me, tell us what she is to you?" Kavya pulled Anshik's legs.

Ananya blushed uncomfortably at the track of the conversation.

'Thank God! Mrs. Dhawan is in the kitchen.'

"Why are you curious, my dear sister?"

"Answer me, *bhaiya*," she cajoled, trying her best to get an answer from him.

"Give me an honest answer and I would relieve you of getting me my Raksha Bandhan gift," she tempted him with an incentive.

"Ananya is my . . ." he paused, building up the suspense.

Two pairs of eyes observed him with the utmost curiosity.

His own confusion prevented him from defining their relationship, as he could not fully comprehend the intensity of his emotions.

"Friend . . ."

"Just a friend?"

"No, my best friend."

"No way."

121

"Why? What did you expect?" he taunted Kavya.

Kavya pouted.

It disappointed Ananya that he termed her as just a friend.

'Not a friend, little fool. Best friend,' her mind corrected her thought. But she longed for more. Irritated by his reply, she took her leave.

"It is almost time and I have to go. My mother would be waiting for me," she informed them.

"I'll drop you. It is late," Anshik volunteered.

"No, my mother has come for shopping at the supermarket, next street. I'll join her. You continue your celebration. I don't want to disturb my friend and take his time."

She stressed the word 'friend' and walked out just like that.

"What is wrong with her?" asked Anshik.

His sister answered, "You should know *bhaiya*, because I have absolutely no idea what is happening between you two."

CHAPTER 12

The Relationship Strengthens

Wash your feet in the sea. Eat ice-creams. Let your hair fly as you take a long drive. Sharing little joys in life with people you like are the memories that you will carry with you till your grave.

Ananya neither called him nor visited their home for the next two weeks. Anshik missed her like hell and ached to see her and hear her voice. He understood that, just like him, Anu wanted more from their relationship. He could have called her but could not give her the clarity until he was settled. She had to wait, and they had all the time in this world. He had to establish himself before making the big move. It was a torture for him, and he missed her crazily. Even Kavya was annoyed by the number of times he inquired about her friend.

"Why don't you call and check?" she blasted him, which he had ignored studiously.

It was Saturday, and he stepped inside, completing his morning workout by eight. His mother and Kavya were busy getting ready to go out.

"Anshik, I have kept your breakfast on the table. I have already given food to papa. We are going to your aunt's house. We will be back by seven in the evening. If you are going out, inform your father and lock the home from outside," instructed Sheela.

"Okay, ma."

"Do you want to join us?" asked his mother.

"No, I don't like Aunt Tara."

"She keeps pestering *bhaiya*, asking about his future," reported Kavya.

"What is wrong with that? She does that because she cares for him," Sheela told them sternly.

Ignoring her comment, Anshik waved them bye and went to his room. "Poor *bhaiya*. You are wrong, ma. He is doing his best. One day, he will reach heights that no one has ever reached."

"I hope so too, Kavya. But you know papa's situation, right? He needs to get operated on fast. Even a loan would help. But who would give us a loan, with no surety?"

"How about this house?"

Sheela was shocked. "Never say that. Without a roof over our head, what will we do? This home is so special to papa. This was the first house he got with his earnings. He is attached to this place. We can't do that. Our only hope is Anshik now."

She let out a sigh.

*****

124

The doorbell rang twice. Anshik answered the door, wondering if his mother and sister had come back. He looked at the clock. It was nine in the morning. Hardly an hour had passed since they left, but he was done with all his morning rituals and was about to have breakfast.

"Ananya . . ."

His eyes feasted on her after two long weeks. His heart rate sped up the moment she was in his vicinity. With mild makeup on, she wore a white flower-patterned maxi dress with her hair let loose. A bindi stood out from the center of her forehead, enchanting him.

"How did you come?"

"Bus, and before you ask me, it took me an hour. Where is Kavya?" She tried her best to avoid him.

"Why? Will you not talk to me?" He blocked her way in. She averted her eyes, though she had already scanned him earlier.

He looked calm and carefree, dressed casually in a black T-shirt and blue shorts.

"We have a presentation to be submitted on Monday and Kavya is my partner. So I came to meet her."

"Did you check with her before you started from your home?"

"No . . ." her sound went in, chiding herself for her foolishness. "What is the problem? Is she not there?" she asked.

"No, she has gone to Aunt Tara's house with ma."

"Oh, I did not know that. Since it is the weekend, I thought she would be here."

Catching his eyes, she told him, "I'll leave then."

"No." His harsh command halted her.

"Come in. You need to travel back for another hour to reach home. Did you have your breakfast?"

She shook her head.

"You will feel weak without food. Ma's *rotis* are tasty. Come in and have some."

Ananya had also missed him badly. The invitation to join him for breakfast tempted her to give in. "Alright."

He heaved a sigh of relief, happy that she accepted his invite.

"Has uncle eaten? Where is he?" she asked in concern.

"As usual in his room. Yes, he has taken his breakfast, and I took him out with the assistance of his wheelchair this morning. He enjoyed the view and now he is resting."

"Happy for him," she confided.

Ananya sat opposite him at the dining table, and he served her a couple of rotis with *chana* masala.

"Yum," she said as she took a bite.

Anshik served himself. "Mother's preparations are exceptional. She is the best cook I have ever seen."

She laughed. "This is the default claim of all the sons in this world. But I don't deny the taste either. Aunty's cooking is excellent."

The rapport they tried to establish did not stay long. An uncomfortable silence took them over.

"What happened, Anu?"

"Nothing."

"Red alert to me. I'll decode your nothing to everything."

"What could be wrong?"

"You neither visited nor called for two weeks."

"A friend need not share her whereabouts all the time," she informed as she glared at him.

126

"Agree but . . ." He held her hand from the other side of the table.

"But?"

"I missed you."

She gasped. She had not expected that confession.

"Every second of the day, I missed you. The idea of visiting your home in Khed Shivapur crossed my mind. Then I remembered what you had told me about your father. He's one of those orthodox individuals who wouldn't be okay with friends coming over, isn't that right? So, I was just hoping that you would come."

"I missed you too," she told him, not wanting to clarify what had triggered her anger.

"Then stay here today. We can spend time together. Anyway, you would have informed your parents that you are visiting Kavya. When are they expecting your return?"

"By six in the evening."

"Plenty of time ahead."

"What? How could I? Your mother and sister are not here."

Meanwhile, they completed their breakfast and washed the plates.

"Are you worried that I'll have my wicked way with you?" he teased.

"No." She bit her lower lip hard to avoid her embarrassment.

"What is your problem, then?"

"Nothing."

Though he teased her, he was perfectly aware of her dilemma.

"My father is right in the next room. Nothing to worry. I'll help you with your presentation."

They worked in tandem for the next one hour. Anshik helped her studiously, as he had promised. She needed someone to edit her work. She had prepared a book review on the classic tale—*Oliver Twist* written by Charles Dickens. Since Anshik had already read that tale, it was easy for him to help her with the editing.

About to close her laptop, she stretched her hands up tiredly, and her attention was disturbed by a small wooden swing.

He looked at the yearning in her eyes.

"You want to play?"

"Yes, please. From the moment I stepped into this house, I have always wanted to play on this swing."

The child in Ananya came out with full throttle. She ran to the swing, forgetting all her troubles, and sat on it.

"Come on, help me swing high."

"What? Are you crazy?" demanded Anshik unbelievingly.

"Please . . . this is a long-time dream of mine."

"But you cannot swing high. This is an indoor swing for God's sake."

"Whatever possible," she agreed.

The ride started on a pleasant note.

While Anshik was pushing the swing from the front, Ananya caught him off guard by accelerating its speed with a push from her legs.

They took a tumble to the floor, along with the folded bed that was kept at the side, after she was thrown out of the swing and landed against him.

With Anshik at the bottom, she was sandwiched between him and the bed.

"Oh gosh, I am sorry. Are you alright?" She tried to get up.

Anshik held her, forbidding her to leave.

She probed his intention with her honey-brown eyes.

Anshik kept staring at her as if he had never seen her before. He did not want her to move as he felt her velvety skin against him. Their hearts thundered, and he breathed in sharply. Having missed her for two weeks, he wound her hands against her hips, locking her securely with him. Their bodies melded together, and he brushed the hair that had fallen on her forehead and tugged it beside her ears.

His electrifying gaze held her rather than his hands, from which she could have come out easily. Tilting his head up, he pressed his lips against hers. She shuddered at his intimate touch, but was surprised. All the kisses they had shared earlier could be termed friendly, and they had never gone this far. The two-week gap had pushed them closer. Destiny was playing an emotional game with them, and she was unsure how it would end. Open-mouthed, he kissed her again, ruffling her glossy hair with his fingers. His other hand tightened his hold, and he kept pressing feathery kisses on her lips again and again and did not want to stop. Her intuition warned her to run away, yet something stopped her.

'But this is all wrong,' her heart pleaded, and she finally forced herself to pull herself a little out of his grip.

"Ansh, Please. This is not right," she beseeched, trying to move away as she gasped for air.

"Relax, lady." He gently loosened his grip and let her get up.

"I did not plan this, Ananya, though I am not sorry that we shared this kiss," he acknowledged.

"Me neither. But that does not mean we can keep kissing again and again."

Though she voiced her denial, both knew that they would treasure their first kiss forever.

"Alright, no more kisses then, but it is going to be difficult," surrendered Anshik.

"My work is done. It is almost eleven. I'll leave. I can't stay here for long."

She continued with a tone of self-righteousness, "That's not right."

Anshik's face fell at her words.

Happy that he had missed her, she pulled his chin up and asked, "We need not stay in. But you can take me out. Won't you, Ansh?"

He laughed. "Your wish is my command, Anu. Let me tell papa I am going out."

After a couple of minutes, they closed the door. Ananya took the backseat of his bike. "Do you remember our last bike ride?" he inquired.

"How could I forget? You drove like mad. For a moment, I thought I was going to die."

He quickly turned to her and covered her mouth, peering into her buttery eyes. "Never say that again. As long as I am around you, I'll never let that happen."

"I know." She smiled.

"Where do you want to go?"

"How about the Broken Trishul temple to start our day?"

"Sure, let us do a round of prayer, for God has gifted us this special day," he professed dramatically.

After visiting the temple, they went to the park, grabbing some coffee along the way. Clicking pictures with their mobile, they knew these memories would stay with them forever.

Together, they enjoyed walking on the lush grass bed after removing their shoes. They found a big swing at the park meant for adults, and he helped her swing high. "Wow!" she screamed in excitement.

"Thank you, Ansh." She gave him a big hug.

After capturing their moments as unforgettable photos, Anshik asked Ananya, "Where next?"

"Have you ever eaten the world's best *panipuri*?"

He shook his head.

"No? Too bad then, Ansh. You have missed something important in your life. Let me take you there," she invited.

She took him to a nearby spot where she had eaten with her friends by the roadside.

Even after he finished eating the mouth-watering snack, he could still taste the flavor of the spicy-sweet liquid, which dripped from the side of his mouth.

Gently, she wiped it, touching his lips.

He sighed.

"For God's sake, don't tempt me, Ananya. We are outside."

"I did not mean to." She pouted.

"Little witch," he admonished with mock anger.

They laughed, unable to control themselves. The gigantic clock at the park gonged five times. It was 5.00 p.m.

"I have to reach my home before six," she told him regretfully.

"Alright, let us leave."

Anshik's voice was sad. She held his hands and whispered, "Today was beautiful. I have never had such fun in my life. I'll never forget this day."

"Me too."

They drove back in silence, remembering every second of the day they had shared. "You can stop here. My home is hardly five minutes away. I can walk," she told him.

Anshik switched off the ignition and removed his helmet.

"Someday, I will not stop here. I will have all the right in this world to drop you at your home, and your father will welcome me."

Moving closer to him, she gently cupped his cheeks. "I know. Hope we have many more days like this in our life," she whispered.

There was an implied consent between them on their relationship, though they never voiced it out.

"You helped me fulfill my sweet dream today."

For a moment, he was confused. "Oh, you are talking about the swing at the park."

"Yes, it is a moment that I will treasure forever and do you know, Ansh? My heart cautions me that this endearing bubble of happiness that we are in might burst anytime. Good things never stay for long. It feels as if we are living in the story that I have created to my liking but will never reach the screens of the people."

Putting his fingers on her lips, he murmured, "Take out the negativity. The bubble of our happiness is in our hands. Despite its fragility, we'll do our best to hold on to it. We both have our own dreams and it's important to fulfill them, not just for ourselves but for our families too. And remember, Ananya . . ."

An intuition told him to warn her. "Life is never easy. Whatever happens between us, hold on to your goals. Your creations will be displayed on screens worldwide, exactly as you desired. Don't give up. People will one day eagerly wait for your new releases. And who knows? You might probably make our story into a movie someday!"

She looked at the confidence he had in her. Even she did not have that on her.

"Your fighting spirit is what I admired about you on the first day we met, and that makes you special. I want you to try, no matter what. Promise me."

"I'll try." She put her hands into his. "Where is your promise?" She questioned.

"You are getting it. Don't worry."

He paused for a second and breathed in. "I promise that soon I will be a CEO of a successful IT company, doing what I love and roll in money. I'll reach the top so that people invite me to attend your special premier show as a chief guest."

"Deal." They shook hands, inspiring each other with love, though they never acknowledged their feelings, driven by their dreams.

Ananya's slippers broke as she turned to leave.

"Oops . . ."

"What happened?"

"A minor mishap. I'll manage."

"See you then."

She took the broken slippers in her hand and walked back barefoot. Though they did not make a big deal out of it, their minds warned intuitively that something terrible was about to disturb their lives.

With remorse, they parted ways as the evening sun slowly sank into the sky and darkness took over. This growing feeling of negativity added to their sorrow as heaviness weighed them down despite the wonderful day they had shared earlier.

CHAPTER 13

Things Fall Apart

Sometimes, when you drive along the bumpy roads of life, things fall apart. Do not stop your drive midway, though. You will never get to know what awaits at your beautiful destination.

It was seven in the evening, and Anshik rang the doorbell. His mother and sister were back, and their slippers were on the front rack. As Kavya opened the door, she warned her brother, "Be prepared, *bhaiya*. Aunt Tara did her job perfectly."

"She kept pointing out to ma that you needed to get a job no matter what for papa's operation."

Heeding Kavya's advice, he kept his face staid and walked in quickly to his room, trying to avoid confrontation with his mother.

"Anshik," she called him firmly. "Come here."

Getting her intent, he understood that evading the query would not help, and he had to sort this out with his mother once and for all and hoped that she would understand his delay.

"You have been job hunting for three years now. I never pushed you for the first two years until your father's accident. But I can't give you the time and space now. You know you have to do what is right for the family."

"Ma . . ." he sighed and continued, "It is not as if I am trying. I have concluded that jobs don't suit me. I want to start my venture."

"Oh God, this is what you have been thinking recently. And here I thought, my son has become responsible and toned down enough to attend the interviews."

"Ma," he sought to argue, but she cut him off.

"I never thought that you would be so selfish. Don't you want your papa to walk again? For how long could we hold off the operation because of this monetary crisis? Tell me."

Her voice was stern, and Anshik felt that there was no point in arguing with her. "Just give me some more time, ma. I am almost there. I am waiting for a loan to be approved to start my company. The clients are ready."

"Loan? If you can get a loan for your start-up, why not for papa's operation?" she screamed.

Kavya tried her best to stop the argument, but it was useless. Tara's indirect complaints had completely influenced her mother. She is jealous of *bhaiya* because her son is not of *bhaiya's* caliber, though he works for a small company and earns 15,000 rupees per month. Whenever she gets an opportunity, she tries her best to turn ma against Anshik *bhaiya*.

"Why can't a mother look through these curtains and see the naked truth and stand against these fake relations?" fumed Kavya.

"Don't you think I had not thought about it, ma? How can you think I am shallow?" There was a genuine pain in his eyes. Sheela's eyes were red and watery, and so was Anshik's.

They had not realized that they were yelling at each other.

"These loans are meager, and Tanvi is trying to help me get it from her father, mostly. The rest I have convinced the other investors to pitch in. For the company, it is five lakh to begin with, whereas for papa's operation, it is 20 lakh."

"So now you have started to compare the amounts, is it?" Sheela was beyond any reasoning.

"I will not answer that, ma . . . you know me. Please, keep your voice down. It is going to disturb papa."

"As if you care about your papa," she taunted him sarcastically.

There was a loud sound from the other room.

Thud.

With a huge cut on his wrist, Ankush fell from his bed.

"Papa!" Anshik ran to him.

Kavya and Sheela followed him.

"Oh God, what happened? Were you so frustrated with the delay in walking on your own that you wanted to take your life?" Sheela cried without a thought.

Ankush's heart shivered at her words.

"No, Sheela, listen. Don't you know about our son? You are torturing him, throwing mud at him."

"Not intentionally."

Anshik stopped both. "That is okay, papa. It is ma who scolded me, and it is okay. But we don't have time to discuss this. Let me take you to the hospital. Why did you do this?" he ended on an aggressive note, holding him in his arms, not expecting an answer in the state of urgent crisis.

"Kavya, call the ambulance," he instructed his sister, who stood shell-shocked at their father's state. His blood was spurting out slowly, though the cut was minor. He was weakening visibly.

Ankush held his son's hands.

"I don't want Sheela to disturb you and put a load of burden on you. It is your career and your life. Don't get influenced by people around you, even if it is your mother. Do what you love, *beta*."

The sound of a siren interrupted them. Kavya ran out to see if the ambulance had come.

"Sheela, sell this house. Nothing is more important than Anshik's career. Don't yell at him. Give him time and show him you are confident that he will succeed, and he will."

His eyes drooped, and he could not continue.

Sheela screamed in desperation. "Am sorry, Ankush . . . please do not leave me. I have no one else. Let me sell the house and sort out the issues. Just be with us."

Ankush fainted as the driver and a couple of attendants rushed in.

*****

Ananya woke up the next day with a lot running through her mind. Somehow, she had to convince her parents to allow her to apply for the filmmaking course for two years. She walked in to see her father video chatting with Sandeep, her brother, who was pursuing his higher studies at Oxford University. Their conversation had stopped her in tracks.

"And I have found the best match for Ananya."

"Oh, is it? Great, papa," he enthused.

"He is a software engineer like you, working in the UK."

"Good for her."

"I had sent them a picture of Ananya. His parents like the bride. What is not to like about her? She is beautiful," her father kept blabbering with enthusiasm.

"The groom is coming next week. If all is fine, we can fix the engagement. She is completing her course this month."

She ran to her mother. "What is papa talking about, ma?"

"Are you not happy, Ananya? Your papa has found someone nice to take care of you. He has studied well and is already established. You could travel the world with him," she exaggerated.

"Ma, why don't you get it?"

Ananya's mother caught her daughter's reluctance.

"What is the problem, *beti*? Don't you want to get married?"

She recollected Anshik's words.

'Life is never easy. Whatever happens in your life, hold on to your dreams. Don't let the rules of society overrule you because you are a girl. Promise me.'

Her willpower to stand up against her parents strengthened.

"I don't need someone to take care of me. I need to get into a position where I can care for myself."

Mrs. Pooja Mehta was astonished at her words.

"Ma, don't you see that half of your problems would have been sorted if you had financial independence instead of depending on papa?"

Her statement was correct, and Pooja could not deny that.

"Ma, I want to be financially independent, chase my dreams, build my career, buy a car and a house, and then marry."

"He will buy you a house and a car, Ananya," Pooja claimed.

"Ma, do you think that is right? Do I have to marry someone to get a house and a car?"

Pooja could understand her daughter's sentiments, and her mind agreed. But she was unsure how her father would react.

"But, Ananya, papa has already said okay to the groom's family."

"No, ma." Her voice was adamant.

Mr. Shashank Mehta walked in. "Ananya . . ."

She swallowed the rest of her thoughts hovering over her lips.

"I hope your mother informed you about the NRI proposal that you have got. The bridegroom is earning handsomely in London in a reputable software company. His parents have already seen your photograph and are happy. The groom, Rahul, is visiting India next week and wants to meet you. If all goes well, we can have a quick engagement ceremony."

Ananya stepped forward. She had to be bold and speak out. If not, she was sure her life would go on a toss.

"Papa . . ."

He turned to her, wondering what her query could be. To him, his arrangement was perfect.

"I don't want to get married now."

"Arre . . . not now, Ananya. I will fix the date for your marriage after you complete your exams."

"Papa, I don't want to marry until I properly set up my career."

"Career? Have you gone mad?"

"Is it wrong for a woman to speak about her career?"

"Did you read a book on feminism recently?" he taunted.

"Is feminism about having a career for women, papa?" She was tired of arguing.

Ignoring her question, he asked in return, "What do you want to take up as your career?"

Not sure how he would react, she talked about her plan for building her career. "I want to do my post-graduation in filmmaking for two years, and I want to create movies or serials someday that people would love."

Her father looked at her as if she had grown horns.

"What is the necessity of a career for a girl? And that, too, as a movie-*wala*?" His lips twirled down in revulsion.

Wearing a white kurta, he looked like an accountant from the rural area.

"Papa, that is my dream . . ."

"Dream? Ananya, are you even listening to yourself? What would our relations say about this?"

"I don't care about them, papa."

"But I do. They will start whispering that you are working for the so-called dirty movie industry . . . but look at the other side. Rahul could give you the best life. He is a wonderful person. I have spoken to him over the phone."

Her father tried his best to convince her in a nicer way.

"Papa, I don't want someone else to give me a better life. I want to create a better life myself."

"By making movies?" He laughed.

"Papa—" With no mood to listen to her any further, he stopped her.

"Enough of your nonsense, Ananya. I don't want to hear any more arguments. I have already given my commitment. Get ready for your wedding. I'll pick up the date and let you know. Be a good girl now."

His ultimate threat sounded scary.

She shook her head.

"Look at her nerves. How dare you show your disobedience, Ananya? Don't you have an ounce of respect for the person who raised you? Is this what I get for permitting you to study?"

"Papa, please," she pleaded.

"Stop your nonsense, Ananya. This is your last warning."

"You can make many threats, papa, but I'll not agree to this marriage. I want to pursue my higher education in digital filmmaking."

Losing his temper, Shashank raised his hand. Pooja stepped in between them.

"No. How can you hit our daughter?"

"Don't call her my daughter," he scolded with revulsion, as if he had a foul taste in his mouth.

Turning back to Ananya, he said, "I'll give you an hour to decide. Stay here, and I assure you, you will have a blissful married life with Rahul. If you talk about pursuing that stupid career again and deny this marriage, I don't want to see your face again. I'll disown you. Remember that. I don't want to be answerable to our aunts and uncles for your stupid behavior."

Dropping that threat, he stormed out of the house.

The next moment, Ananya fell on her knees and sobbed. Her mother came near and ruffled her head gently. She looked up to see her pain reflected in her mother's eyes.

"Don't worry, *beti*. Initially, I thought your father would be angry, and Rahul sounded like a decent guy. But after hearing you out, I believe what you told your father is right. Every girl needs to be financially independent."

Ananya stood surprised as her mother continued, "With over twenty-five years of marriage with your father, I am tired of depending on him for everything. I wanted to become a teacher, and your grandfather told me I could become one

142

after marriage. But your father overruled my desire and never allowed me to become one. All I do is cook and clean the whole day. Thinking of it, I have lost all my wishes and dreams along this grubby path. I don't want the same for you."

She realized that Pooja had been hiding her pain all along.

"Ma . . ."

"Time to move, *beti*."

She packed the baggage with her dresses and thrust a wad of money in her hands.

"I have seen your father for years, Ananya. He will not change. To him, a girl is meant only for marriage and to take care of the home. He does not think that we have our own desires. But don't let that stop you. Go, Ananya. Chase your dreams. I want to see your beautiful creations on the screen. My blessings will always be with you."

"Thanks, ma, for believing in me."

*****

CHAPTER 14

Pain of Separation

Holding on to the mind-numbing pain of your broken heart is addictive, but hopeless. Untangle yourself from the web of emotion because life moves on no matter what happens in and around you.

With a bag in her hand, she took a bus from Khed Shivapur to Pune. Her mind kept contemplating her next move. Should she find a hostel near her college until she completes her exams?

She also had to talk to Anshik about their future, unaware of the scenario at his home. There was no response from him after she had called him twice. She was stuck in a desperate situation, and she had to talk to him. She decided to meet him in person, and holding her bag, she knocked at his door.

No one came out, and she noted the door was locked from the outside. She kept calling Kavya, and she did not pick up her phone either.

'*Where has everyone gone?*' she pondered.

As she was about to leave after a couple of minutes, she saw him parking his bike at the front. "Anshik!" She waved, forgetting her troubles for a moment.

He acknowledged her vaguely but did not smile. His face appeared pale and tense. He did not even inquire if she was waiting for them. Wordlessly, he unlocked the door and let her in as if he was an automated robot.

"Are you alright, Ansh?" she asked, touching his shoulders gently.

Her touch brought him a little to his senses, but he did not meet her eyes. He saw her packed bags when he was about to reply.

"What happened? Why have you brought your bags?"

"I came to talk about that—"

She stopped unsure of his response. With his father out of the danger zone, Anshik felt a little better, though many things disturbed his peace of mind. He had come home to take additional dresses for his mother and sister. Their hospital stay had been extended to support their dad's recovery.

He had asked his friend Tanvi to come home meanwhile. She wanted to talk about the loan he had requested earlier and help them sell their house with her father's support.

With the money Tanvi's father forwards, he would settle the bill for the current predicament of his papa. With the leftover fund, he still needed more for his spine operation, though.

He looked at his watch. "I have little time, Ananya. Be quick. I am waiting for someone," he told her, thinking about the horrifying hours at the hospital.

His thoughts were about his father, who was surrounded by tubes all over and an oxygen mask fixed on his mouth. He also remembered the promise that he had made to his mother and stiffened. Ideally, he did not even have the right to speak with Ananya. That thought ripped his soul, and a strange fear of losing her took over him.

"I will not take much time, Ansh."

Sensing his urgency, she quickly narrated the emotional drama played by her father yesterday.

"I don't want to get married now."

"Fine."

"And I thought I'll take up a hostel next to college for a few days."

"Okay." His monosyllables made her mad.

"Will you help me find a good hostel?"

"Alright, I will help."

"What happened, Ansh? You never speak this way to me. Is something wrong?" she demanded.

About to tell her about his father's reaction yesterday, he thought for a moment rationally. There was no point in overloading her troubles when she herself was in a mental trauma.

"Nothing." He shook his head.

Before his brain could process her troubles and come up with a reasonable solution, she blasted.

"Come on, Ansh . . . here I am, pouring all my troubles to my lover and he responds this way!" she told him dramatically, without getting the seriousness of his situation.

"What did you call me?"

He was shocked to the core.

She blushed. "I did not mean to. I thought I would not call you my love until you propose."

She told him as if she expected his proposal anytime. If she had given him this green signal yesterday, he would have shouted with elation, but today it upset him badly.

"Ananya—"

She put her hands up to stop him. "I know you love me, but you are denying your feelings toward me."

Oh God . . . he did not want this confrontation now.

He could not stop running through the scene in his mind that had happened when his father was inside the ICU yesterday.

His mother's words came back to taunt him. She did what she thought was good for him, and he had fallen right into that in the name of sacrifice. Was he right or wrong? He did not know. Was his mother right then? He did not know that either. He knew only one thing. His heart had broken into pieces after that, and he felt like a walking corpse ever since.

"It will not help even if we sell the house. We will use a little now to settle his current bill, and the remaining amount will not be sufficient. We are still short of money for his spinal operation," wailed Kavya, losing all her hope.

With eyes filled with tears, Sheela Dhawan turned to her son.

She wanted him to succeed desperately and bring the required money. A fire of anguish burnt in her eyes. No matter what, Anshik had to succeed, for all their sakes. He was their only hope.

But his attention was elsewhere as she saw him looking at his ringing mobile. The name flashed—"Ananya Jaan".

"Jaan?"

Sheela was furiously angry. Her son does not need any distractions in his life at present. His focus should only be on his career.

"Anshik!" she screamed.

"Ma . . ."

"Promise me. Your dad was ready to make the ultimate sacrifice for you. He is struggling to survive, trying to support your choice. I agree with your father's words. I'll not push you to go for a job just for the sake of money. Both of us will wait for you to do what you love and succeed. But for that to happen, don't you think you must put your complete attention into your start-up if you want your vision to work?"

"What or who is deviating me, ma?"

"Ananya."

"No way."

"I have eyes, *beta*. She is your distraction. And I don't blame you either, as this is highly common at your age."

"What are you suggesting?"

"You know."

He gazed at her blankly.

"It is time to break up."

"Ma—"

"Do you want her to suffer with you?"

"No."

"How would you take care of her then with no job and overloaded with responsibilities?"

He did not have an answer.

"You can't and your foremost responsibility is your father, who is fighting for his life inside that ICU. Am I right?"

He nodded.

"Then promise me that you will leave behind everything that will hinder your growth. Work only on your goals and build your dreams. Succeed. Earn your money . . . not for me but for your father, who is dying slowly."

"Promise me."

He stood reluctantly.

"I know that giving up Ananya would be difficult for you. But please . . . if she loves you truly, she might even wait for you in the future, and I promise you I'll not stand against your love after your success. But making her wait forever would ruin her future, *beta*. Think of her as well. Let her live her life. You live yours. Make your father walk again . . . the sooner, the better."

She fell on his legs.

"Ma." He lifted her up and drowned in her teary eyes.

"I promise." His lips shivered.

"On your father's life?"

He nodded with tears in his eyes.

"Anshik . . ." Ananya's voice brought him back to the present.

He wanted to hug her and say that he loved her crazily and things would be alright soon. He wanted to give in to their soulful relationship.

But he could not tell her what he felt. His inner thoughts battled with him intensely. He could not stop them. He tried to turn away from her, but she did not let him, and she kept him captive. Her eyes began overruling his rational thoughts. The '*yes*' hovered on the tip of his tongue.

'*Don't give in, Anshik. Your mother is right. How could you commit yourself to any relationship in your present situation? Your father is struggling for his life,*' his inner mind tormented him.

'Supporting you all the way till he fainted, you are now doubly responsible for making him well and walk again. He deserves that. Right now, you don't have a steady job, nor your loan is approved to begin your start-up. Even if you could convince Tanvi to get the money, it would take time to establish your company and earn back what you have borrowed. Once you are done repaying that amount, you still have to get back the house that would be sold to pay the hospital bill. You still need money for the operation. And, most of all, you promised ma . . . on your papa's life.

His conscience tore him in two. Like many other men of his age, at twenty-four, his overloaded responsibilities swallowed him. His shoulders drooped with regret, and he put his head down a little, unable to meet her eyes.

He had to let her go. His body went rigid at that. He knew he loved her to the core. But his mother was right. He could not give her the happiness she deserved. He had neither the money nor the time to support her at present, and he could not guarantee a happy future either.

And it would be unfair to ask her to wait. She needs to move on, and he will force her to do the same, even if she hates him in return. He would do anything to secure her future and keep her happy, even without him.

"What is running through your mind, Anshik?" she asked him urgently as he had gone into his own world of silence, sensing that he was about to reject her.

Words failed him as he looked into her eyes.

"I am not talking about marriage, Ansh. I am not ready," she clarified.

Getting no answer from him, she had a weird sense of fear threatening to take over her. She caught hold of his shirt collar and demanded, "Answer me."

He made his face blank-devoid of emotion and asked her coolly, "When did we ever speak of love?"

She stood shell-shocked at his query. But he continued, "Did I ever tell you I loved you at any point in time, Ananya?"

Her eyes welled up with tears, and she had a choking sensation inside her throat. She looked at him disbelievingly, and Anshik could feel the pain in her eyes.

But he could neither give her false hope nor ask her to wait for him for n number of years, without knowing what could be this 'n'.

He hardened his heart. "Don't you recollect what I said to my sister when she asked about you?"

Ananya stared at him as a heaviness took over her.

Holding his breath, he said, "I told everyone that you are my best friend. You still are, Ananya. But read nothing more than that."

"Friend? You told me you missed me," she fought back with the rest of the energy left.

"Yes, you did not speak with me, and I missed my best friend," he argued.

"And you kiss your friends?" She threw him away as she left the hold on his collar.

'No, I don't and you mean a lot to me, Anu.'

He wanted to cry, but he did not.

'Not really. You were there at the right time and the right place. You know what happens if cotton is kept closer to the fire,' he taunted her, though it killed him to do so. But this would ensure that she would move on.

She gasped at his insult.

"Enough," she screamed. "I never expected this from you, Mr. Anshik Dhawan. Don't you dare to degrade what we shared. And I am a fool . . . a real fool for believing in you."

She took her bag hurriedly.

"What about your hostel?" he asked her worried.

"I can manage. Do not worry." She threw his request back at him furiously.

"Anshik." Tanvi walked in, as they had forgotten to close the main door with all this drama.

Seeing him, she ran to him and gave him a big hug.

"Oh, dear, I am ecstatic. I told about your proposal to father, and he is okay and has given a green signal to go ahead . . ."

"Oh really, thank you so much!" He hugged her back with delight. The hug they shared told her what he wanted to convey to her. She was just a friend to him. And his love interest was someone else—this lovely little Tanvi, whom he had proposed to, and her father had given his blessing as well. She was late.

A strange feeling of disappointment took over Ananya, but it gave her the strength to walk away from him.

Anshik saw her walking away with tears in his eyes. "I am sorry," he whispered. *Please don't leave me . . .'* his heart pleaded with her.

*****

He closed the diary. But his mind was still connected with their past. His heart had grieved to let her go but from that point in his life, he pushed himself harder and translated all his pain into work.

With luck on his side, his loan got approved with Tanvi's help. He worked day and night as if a demon haunted him.

He arranged the rest of the money for his father's operation within months. It took him another two years to repay all his loans and get back their lost home. And this last year, he made a tremendous profit, extending the wings of his business. This was what he had dreamt of, but he had lost Ananya in this process.

They had their difficulties, but she still did not know why he had to let her go and he did not want to tell her either, raking mud against his mother. He knew Ananya had lost her trust in him years ago. And he had to fight for her and win her back. This was the self-inflicted punishment he had given him for hurting her. Going to her and pleading with her with a sob story did not appeal to him.

Also, professing his love out of the blue might disturb her journey toward her dreams. He has reached his milestone as they had promised, but she had not started off still. No matter what happened between them, he would definitely stand with her on her journey.

'That is my promise to you, Ananya . . .'

He was heading a huge IT company because of her simple suggestion and the right guidance at the right time. And most of all, she stuck with him when he had absolutely nothing. And this was his time to repay everything to her.

'Though you want to do that, you are scared, Anshik!' His heart laughed at him.

"No, am not!" he screamed.

'Yes, you are. Your heart aches at the thought of being tagged as a friend by her. Don't cheat yourself. You long for more, but you are worried that she might retaliate and hurt you the way you hurt her earlier.'

His heart's musing was right. He was scared that she would fling his feelings back at him, the same way he had done.

CHAPTER 15

Advertisement Opportunity

Sometimes we are reluctant to stand up after the fall, frightened that we would fall again. Letting that fear dominate us would keep us in the pit of darkness forever.

Ananya had left Kavya's home the next morning after the eventful weekend, intending to avoid Anshik. But the moment she stepped into the office, Anil told her that the CEO, Mr. Anshik Dhawan, had asked her to meet him.

"What for?" she had asked, reluctant to see him after her confrontation with him about why he had left her earlier. She cringed at her query. What had made her ask that? She knew that he would not answer her. He had not done it years ago, nor was he going to do it now.

'*I am to blame for creating an awkward situation between us, despite an easy rapport we shared recently,*' she thought.

"No idea." Anil shook his head. "Don't worry, I have asked Gagan to take care of the vending machine."

"Thanks, Anil." She left with a tray of coffee.

Ananya stepped into his cubicle after formally knocking at the door.

"Yes."

"Good morning, Anshik."

He took his eyes off the laptop and said, "Morning, Ananya. Please take a seat."

His tone was highly formal; he made it obvious that he didn't want to hear any arguments from her and that she could not afford to displease him at the office.

She passed him the cup of coffee.

He gave her a couple of printed sheets before taking a sip from the cup.

"What is this?"

"You know to read, right?" he taunted her.

Glaring at him, she gave a quick glance. It was a call for directing and writing the script for the new advertisement for TechWarriors.

Her initial excitement to see that piece of information waned as her mind pulled her down, recalling that her mother had left her forever.

'*I can never be a filmmaker. I am going to fail anyway, even if I give my best shot. Something or the other will happen and spoil this opportunity. Such is my bad luck. Even if I win, who will I celebrate with? My mother—the only soul who had supported me in the family—is no more . . .*'

Her negativity sucked her into a web of darkness without letting her think rationally. She passed the papers back.

"This has nothing to do with me," she denied politely and continued, "If you have got nothing else for me, I'll leave."

With that note, she got up from her chair.

"I am not done with you, Ananya. Take your seat." He pushed her back harshly.

"Okay, boss," she retorted sarcastically and sat back.

"Do you even realize that the sheet of paper you threw back at me is your golden ticket to your dream?"

She knew it, but her mind was wary of trying it. She had to give him a reason, though.

"I don't want any favoritism, just because you consider me your friend."

"Who told you I am offering you this opportunity?" he asked her.

She went blank.

"I am a businessman, Ananya. I prioritize what benefits me the most. A request will be posted in the newspaper tomorrow, urging interested individuals to email our marketing team. Additional instructions would be provided to them for preparing the script. A team of professionals would choose the best out of the lot, headed by my marketing lead."

She could understand how Anshik ran such a big company smoothly. He had a sharp business acumen, not driven by emotions.

Not getting a reply from her, he added, "I told you earlier that I am not running a charity. This ad needs to bring in additional business for me and create a good branding for my company amongst the public, as it is relatively a new one."

"This has nothing to do with me," she told him again, not wanting to take part. Her mother's loss dominated her, and she had no time for anything else. A dull throbbing pain inside screamed at her that she was still alive in this world, whereas her mother had lost her opportunity even to survive.

"You don't have a choice. I want you to contact the marketing department regarding this advertisement. Get the script ready."

"Are you forcing me to do something that I don't want to do?"

Anshik was furious at her question. He stood up from his chair and went near her. She got up as he grabbed her shoulders, turned her toward him, and demanded, "Look into my eyes when you tell me that this does not interest you."

"Yes, I am not interested," she claimed, looking elsewhere.

"Don't lie. I can read you like an open book."

"You are hurting me," she whimpered. Anshik noted the red marks he had made on her arms.

"I am sorry for being rough. I didn't mean to. But what you are doing makes little sense to me."

"I might work for you, Anshik. But you can't push me back to filmmaking again."

"I have read your scripts earlier, Ananya. And I don't want the industry to lose a gem like you."

"I don't care about them," she denied vehemently.

There was a knock at the door. Taking his chair again, he said, "Come in."

Tanvi stepped in.

"Hello, Anshik. Thanks for making me a part of your jury to choose the best ad for your company."

Ananya was dumbfounded to see her after three years. Why was she not married to Anshik when her father had given the green signal for their relationship? That was her understanding when she had left.

She had wanted to ask him about Tanvi multiple times but could not bring her into the conversation, just like that when she had declared that he was a friend. He did not want to make him suspicious that she was still holding a torch for him.

She had not seen Tanvi since her comeback, and she thought that their relationship was broken already, but it did not appear so.

'*And Tanvi is a part of the jury!*' Her heart pained as she thought of the way Anshik had chosen Tanvi over her, three years back despite the special bond they had shared.

In a beautiful blue gown, she looked slender and elegant. Her round face and dimples made her appear gorgeous. Her perfume had notes of cherry, and it was pleasant. Ananya felt positively dowdy in her yellow kurti, which she had matched with a simple black pant. With her bare face, she felt she was no match for her bubbliness.

Tanvi stood near Anshik, who was dressed well in a three-piece grey suit, and to any onlooker, they would have made a beautiful pair. That thought triggered her pain.

When Tanvi noted Ananya, she remarked, "I have seen you somewhere."

"Yes, you have. Tanvi, meet Ananya, the facility manager and Kavya's friend and college mate once upon a time."

"Ah, now I remember. I have seen you at Anshik's home."

"And, Ananya, this is Tanvi, my right-hand man, or should I say woman? She has always been there for me whenever I needed her."

"Happy to help you, dear," Tanvi beamed at the compliment.

Not wanting to hear their conversation anymore, Ananya turned to him. "I will leave then."

"Yes, please . . . we have got plenty to discuss. It has been a long time since I have seen Tanvi. And make sure that you submit your entry as well," he spoke boss-like.

She retorted, "As you please, sir."

Anshik laughed internally at her tone.

"By the way, can you please bring a cup of coffee for Tanvi? She would be tired coming from the other end of Pune in this heavy traffic just for us."

"Anything for you, Ansh," agreed Tanvi.

"Sure, sir. Anything else?" Ananya asked furiously.

"Yes, please ask my PA Ravi to book a table for lunch at Hotel Tree-Star for two."

"Who are you going with?" The question was out before she could control herself.

"Of course, with Tanvi. Who else?" His confirmation made her angry, and she stormed out of his room.

*****

She called Vaishnavi at the cafeteria and informed her, "Mr. Anshik Dhawan has a guest. Could you please serve her coffee?"

"Sure, Ananya." She nodded. Avoiding seeing them together did not calm Ananya, though.

How dare you, Anshik?' She hit her hands on the table aggressively.

'Oh God, what is wrong with me? He is just a friend. Hmmm . . . then why can't I digest the fact that he is going for lunch with his girlfriend or ex-girlfriend?'

Her mind confirmed weakly that no matter what happened

between them, she could not see him with anyone else. She gazed out of the enormous glass window of the cafeteria.

Was she still in love with him, despite how much he had hurt her in the past? She could not find any other answer to her jealousy, which tattered her.

Anshik took Tanvi to his car with his hands on her hip. Not wanting to see them together, she tried to turn her attention to the Excel sheet, doing her best to tally the count of coffee for that month.

But it was not possible. Though irrational, she could not control her increasing temper. An hour and a half passed.

She tortured herself by conjuring images of Anshik taking Tanvi into his arms. She clenched her fist and wanted to confirm if they were back at the office after their lunch. Or worse, were they romancing the restaurant till now? How could she stop the resentful thoughts that tore her soul?

Throwing away caution, she took the lift and ran to his cubicle to check on him. Without knocking, she barged in to see him working on his laptop alone.

"Ananya? I don't remember calling you." He frowned.

"I came to pick—"

Before completing her stuttering, she looked around. The cabin was empty apart from them. "Where is Tanvi?"

He was perplexed. "Tanvi? Why should she be here? She is not an employee."

"Yes, but she is your girlfriend, right? Hence, I expected her to be here."

"You came to check the whereabouts of my girlfriend, is it?" he asked her incredulously.

She was caught by his question and tried to manage.

"How does it even matter to me, Anshik? I came here to pick up the paper that you showed me earlier. You forced me to take part, right?"

Feeling a little better that nothing had happened as she had imagined, she bent closer to take the paper that fluttered on his desk.

"Oh, gosh . . ."

"What?"

"I can smell Tanvi's perfume on you."

With those words, she tried to run away from his cubicle.

Anshik was quick to block her against the door. "What do you mean, Ananya?"

"You have kissed her," she accused.

He neither accepted nor rejected her accusation.

Holding her hands, he pulled her close to him. He sandwiched her between the cabin door, locking her effectively.

She was not going away without giving proper answers.

"Why does it matter to you if I kiss her?"

"No, it does not." She could not look into his eyes.

"I don't think so. I see the green monster of envy peeping out of you. You wanted me to be your friend. And I repeat, why should you feel anything if I kiss my girlfriend?"

Every time she heard him acknowledge Tanvi as his girlfriend, a feeling of despair gnawed at her slowly.

"Do you kiss your friend and your girlfriend on alternate days? Are kisses not reserved for someone special in your diary? You kissed me a couple of days back and now you have . . ." She paused.

"What do you think I did with Tanvi?" he questioned intensely.

She tried to ward off her irrational jealousy.

'What he did with Tanvi should not matter to me.' She reiterated the same to her heart, which refused to obey strictly.

He eyed her, awaiting her reply.

"Do you think I did this?"

He trailed his fingers down her cheeks, and her skin pricked at his mesmerizing touch. The mild vanilla fragrance that emanated from her taunted him, and it magnified his desire triple-fold as he held her tightly, draping his other arm around her hips.

His breath blended with hers. Every sane thought in her head vanished. All it mattered now was his touch, which kindled warmth everywhere, spreading a glow. He turned her a little to the back and traced the side of her neck, and a pulling sensation took over her. His lips trailed on the same path tentatively. Gently, he pushed away the hair that obstructed his fluttering kisses.

She closed her eyes, sinking into the passionate web he wove around her. Her breathing became highly erratic. His hands leisurely traced the sides of her shoulders. Turning her back, he drowned in her eyes.

"Open your eyes, Anu," he murmured.

As if his wish was her command, her eyebrows fluttered. Caught in his sensual snare, her hand speared into his hair.

"Ansh, please."

Her other palm was pressed against his chest. He lifted her slightly against the closed door in one graceful yet powerful movement.

Her lips trembled. Perfectly shaped like a bow, they invited him to taste the sweetness. And with that intent, he moved closer, until there was no space between them.

"Should I stop, Anu?"

Caught in the moment, she did not reply.

"Please don't ask me to stop," he pleaded.

She covered the gap between their lips, conveying her desire, and hooked her hands around his shoulders. The moment he got her consent, his eyes were on fire.

He nipped at her top lip sensually, pulling it lightly between his own. He could feel her softness, and his senses were blown away by that electrifying connection.

Dropping her down, he urgently cupped her cheeks and claimed her lips back. He knew that this was the moment he had longed for unconsciously. He felt as if they were establishing the connection between their souls again. She whimpered a little, and he took a step back to look at her dazed face. Her eyes appeared hazy, as if someone had drugged her.

'*Oh God . . . this is not the right time,*' his mind warned him.

'*She has mountains to climb, dreams to achieve, and he has to stand by her. And this passion of theirs will not help them.*'

But he gathered her closer, not wanting to let her go.

"Ananya," he whispered.

She felt as if someone was waking her up from a beautiful dream.

He shook her gently from her trance.

"Ansh—"

"We need to stop, Ananya. This is not the right moment for us."

Embarrassed, she nodded obediently. He was right.

"Do you regret what we did, Anu?"

She shook her head, unable to say a word. She did not have any regrets.

"Good."

He kissed her forehead once more before he let her go.

CHAPTER 16

Pooja's Letter

Bad phases in life are okay. It shows how tough you are and brings out the powerhouse of your mental strength you never thought existed within you.

Ananya consciously avoided Anshik for the rest of the week. She was afraid that he would guess that what she felt for him was beyond friendship. No friend would become possessive the way she did. No matter what he felt for her, she knew that she had always loved him. But her luck did not help her. He caught her in the lift alone. She averted her eyes as he turned to her.

"What is your problem, Ananya? You told me you don't regret what happened between us."

"I don't."

"Does not look like that. You are running scared."

She frowned at his claim. "I am not."

"You are."

His words made her ponder.

'Yes, I am scared. Afraid that you might hurt me again, as I am losing my heart to you, bit by bit.'

Inside the elevator, he pulled her once and kissed her quickly on her lips before she could react and taunted her, "Now go, run faster."

Losing her balance, she fell on his chest, and their bodies collided. The intimate contact lasted for a few seconds, but it was enough for Ananya to trigger her feelings. She needed to stay apart from him at whatever cost until she was sure of Anshik's feelings.

She kept instructing herself that this was not the right thing to do. He had already broken her heart once.

Yes, she knew that he would do anything for her, but not even once had he told her that what he felt for her was beyond friendship.

Hence, it is better to stay within her bounds. Behaving like a jealous wife when she was with him would get her nowhere.

The lift door opened, disrupting her thought, and she ran away from him as if she was on fire as a couple of bystanders looked at them curiously.

The rest of the week went uneventful, but work was hectic. And in her spare time, she tried to write the script for the advertisement after getting the guidelines from the marketing team lead. She could not come up with anything good.

The moment she tried writing, memories of her mother haunted her and blocked her thinking. She felt as if she was responsible for her death.

Had she not gone back home asking her mother for money, she would not have become stressed and worried about her.

That thought taunted her. She had inadvertently caused her depression and triggered the downfall of her mother's health, which ultimately took her life.

As a penance, she thought she should stop writing scripts or think about making movies. She could not sleep properly with the pain building in her heart gradually day by day.

They had shared a beautiful bond, and she missed her like hell. The past few years were hard for her, as they had to stay away because of her father. But inside, she knew that her mother was somewhere around, and the thought that she would make her proud had kept her going. But now everything had changed.

She longed for the maternal support that Pooja had always given her. She wanted to feel her hug and sleep on her lap, throwing away her worries to the gutter.

Missing her mother badly, Ananya woke up on Saturday. She had successfully avoided Anshik at the office, but somewhere inside, she missed him too. Loneliness haunted her. They were the two most important people in her life.

The shrill noise of the mobile stopped her flow of thoughts.

"Who could call me on a Saturday morning?" she croaked as she picked up to see the caller.

'Oh, it is Anshik!'

A slight tinge of excitement crept inside her, despite her melancholic mood.

'Is he calling her to continue the conversation that was cut abruptly in the lift? Should I ignore or pick up his call?'

Her sane mind told her to ignore it, but her heart longed to pick up the call. This was the first time he had called her personal number since they met again.

"Hello."

"Anshik, here." His tone was crisp, boss-like.

'*As if I did not know.*' She looked at the screen comically.

"Yes, tell me, Anshik. Is this an official call?"

"Do you want to report to work on Saturday?"

"If it is not an official call, let me disconnect."

"Don't." His voice was stern.

"I think you are taking advantage of me, Ananya. In terms of work, I take slippages seriously."

"What are you talking about?"

"This is an official call, and I want to meet you. Not at the office, but at the Parkspace restaurant. Be there sharply by nine. Let us discuss things over breakfast."

With that message, he disconnected the call.

"On what?"

Ananya realized she was talking to thin air. Time had passed, but his arrogance remained intact. She fumed with irritation. It was eight in the morning. She hardly had an hour to get ready.

"You are a tyrant, Anshik," she muttered and got up.

*****

He waited for her at the restaurant.

"Anshik."

Turning to her, he complained, "You are late by ten minutes and twenty-three seconds."

"Not all people have a Benz car handy. I took a sharing-auto to reach here."

"That should never be a reason for not being punctual. You should have started early."

She was highly irritated. Ignoring his taunt, she asked him, "What is so important that it needs to be sorted on a Saturday morning? I am a facility lead in the company."

"Let us order first before you start your fight."

His comment made her appear childish. She ignored the temptation to throw the water bottle at him.

"I'll have an omelet and a vegetable sandwich," he turned to the server, unaware of her mental turmoil.

"It is *aloo-paratha* for you, right?" he questioned her. It surprised her that he remembered her favorite dish. But she did not give in.

"Not really. I am not the same Ananya as I was earlier. I'll get the same as you."

He gave her an odd look.

"That's what I wanted to discuss with you. I am glad that you brought it up yourself."

She frowned. "What about me not being the same, gullible Ananya? You told me you called me for some official work."

Anshik could not get past the invisible barrier that she was determined to hold on to. She had an unapproachable look and was dressed in a blue kurti with black leggings. Her hair was neatly pinned up at the top, projecting a professional image.

In contrast, he wore a white sweatshirt with black jeans. His shades were hanging at the front.

He threw a red file at her. "I did not expect this from you."

Ananya's face contorted in confusion. "Open it," he instructed.

She was speechless to see her partly written scripts, which she had crumpled and kept on her desk. She had meant to dispose it but had forgotten.

"I am asking you the same question. Where is the Ananya I knew?"

Before she could reply, he dragged the file from her hands again and flipped through the pages quickly.

"This is pathetic," he criticized.

"I know. That is why I wanted to throw them into the dustbin."

"The Ananya I knew was a great script writer. But I hardly see any traces of her."

"You forced me to write when I had a mental block. I did not want to."

"And hence this pathetic attempt. Well done, Ananya." His tone was sarcastic.

She twisted her lips negatively. "What else did you expect?"

"Years ago, I met a girl with a spark in her eyes. She had a winning spirit, and she pushed not only her but others around her. She fought with her family to stick to her dreams. Her scripts were touching and gripping. And she never stopped trying until she made them perfect. She weaved beautiful stories even for the annual day functions at her college. Where is she?"

"I don't know. Even I can't seem to find her," she told him dejectedly.

"She is right inside you and you don't want to bring her out."

"Oh God, you don't understand. I tried. I really tried. But the moment I try writing, I feel that I have wronged my mother."

"Don't talk rubbish, Ananya. I am sorry for your loss. But you can't use that as a reason for your poor scripts."

The server brought their trays and put them on the table. He gave Ananya an odd look as her eyes welled up with tears.

"Had I stayed at home instead of going behind my dreams, my mother would not have gotten stressed, and she would be alive today. And this guilt is consuming me when I try to write something."

"Don't tell me you believe the story that your brother threw out at you the other day?"

"It is not a story," she argued.

"Don't you get it, Ananya? Your brother was upset with your mother's death and threw mud at you looking for a scapegoat."

"How do you know that? It might be the truth after all."

"I had a nice long talk with him once he came back to the office."

She gasped.

"And he had something with him, which ideally should be with you."

She looked at him, a little shocked.

"I believe he regrets he did not support you earlier, Ananya."

"Don't give me that story, Anshik. Not even once has he supported me or took a stand for me against my father."

"That gives him all the more reason to regret."

"Your mother did not die of stress, as he claimed. He quoted your father's angry words because your mother had fainted after you left last time. She was sick after that, but no one made any effort to take her to the hospital. Everyone thought she had a gastric issue when she complained of chest pain."

Ananya shook her head with regret.

"Oh my God! Ma." She wailed.

"And when your father finally realized that she was seriously sick, he took her to the hospital, but it was too late.

Her reports revealed that she had coronary artery disease, which had led to heart failure. From what he said, I think that your mother had sensed that she would leave this world soon with her deteriorated health."

"How do you say that?" Her voice choked, and she felt as if a ball of iron was stuck in her throat, which refused to move stubbornly. Her eyes were wet with tears of pain and regret.

Your brother found this in your mother's trunk. He passed on the hand-written letter to her.

My dear Ananya baby . . . the letter began. She could not control herself, and she whined inaudibly. She caught the letter with a trembling hand.

Anshik pushed the chair closer to her and held her other hand supportively, lending his strength. She looked at him like a wounded child, and he prompted her, "Go ahead. Read it."

I am sorry, dear. Unfortunately, I couldn't help you out with the money on that day. I feared your father. All my life, I have been the same way. I failed to support you when I should have—

"You did, ma," she whispered.

You were never an argumentative child nor demanded anything from me. All you asked was to have a career of your choice, and I could not help you even with that. That is the biggest mistake I'll carry to my grave. I feel sick, and my instincts tell me I don't have many days to live. I am not sure if I'll be able to meet you again. Your father has restricted me from calling you over mobile. Hence, I am writing what I have to tell you.

Taking a moment or two to calm herself, she continued reading the letter.

When I realized that I don't have many days left, I started regretting a lot of things I should have done in my life, when I had time. I wanted to be a teacher, Ananya. I should have never let my father, nor your father, ruin my dreams. Being a woman, I gave up my happiness and desire, trying to be a dutiful daughter or a good wife. I thought I was pleasing them. But in making them happy, I lost my happiness. I wish that I could have spent one day in my life as a teacher, doing what I love. This is the same case with a lot of other women who bury their dreams for family. Some do it willingly and I am not against it. Being a mother and taking care of my family made me happy too. But I longed to have my identity. I wanted people to call me Pooja teacher instead of treating me as Shashank's wife. I regret that your father's ideologies overshadowed my entire life. The worst part is that I let the same happen to you, Ananya.

To Ananya, it appeared as if her mother was speaking loud to her, and it crushed her mentally.

Please don't repeat the same mistake I made, beti. Being a woman, I agree you would face a lot of hurdles in the future. There might be mountains to move and tougher phases to cross. But remember that no matter what happens, do not give up ever. And do you remember our last conversation before I sent you away? That is my last regret. I told you I'll watch your creations on the screen in the future, and I regret that even that desire of mine could never come true. Not because you could not do it. I know you can, and you will. It is just that I'll not be there to see it.

Holding the paper against her chest, she controlled the emotions which threatened to overflow.

But that should never stop you, Ananya. I don't want you to lead a life full of regrets like the way I did. Do what makes you happy. Chase your dreams. Make your life worthwhile. Try what you want. Don't worry about what people will say. Fail . . . it is okay if you fail. At least you would know that you have tried. Get up and try again. Doesn't matter if you fail once more. Who cares? Your failures are training you, strengthening you. When you look back, you should see a life of beautiful memories and not a life of regrets.

Her words inspired her.

And I'm confident that my daughter will be a successful film director someday and my blessings would always be with you, Ananya dear. The day you achieve your dreams would be the day I would be proud. Will you make me proud, dear? It would wash away all the regrets I had in my life, and I would find peace then!

She broke down completely and sobbed. It did not matter that she was in a hotel with people around.

Clenching the letter tightly, she told Anshik, "I never knew that she felt this way."

He put his other hand over her shoulders to stop her from crying.

Wiping her eyes, she turned to him. Her mother's words added strength to what Anshik had told her earlier.

"I will never give up, Ansh. Watch out."

Anshik smiled and thrust a piece of paper back to her.

She opened the partly crumpled sheet. "Start living again."

It was the same sheet of paper she had given to him years ago.

A smile of gratitude tugged her lips up.

"I will."

"And I will wait for your script for the company advertisement," he reminded her.

"Okay, sir," she dragged with a laugh.

CHAPTER 17

The Comeback

*Your positivity is the only astra which can destroy
the demon of your mental barriers. Once the fences
fall apart, the haze covering the success-pathway
clears, and the road becomes visible.*

As Pooja's words sank within, her older self came out on its own accord. She vigorously prepared scripts for the advertisement that weekend. With a mini heater she had at her hostel, she made black coffee. The powerful potion of caffeine was magic that stimulated her creativity and kept her awake even during the night. She dedicated every second of her weekend to her passion. Her mobile pinged as she kept the coffee cup down, which was almost empty.

"Your cup of coffee would be empty now. Time for a refill. Hope your script is shaping up well."

Anshik's message popped as a notification.

She smiled. He kept sending messages the entire weekend. That made her feel that he was with her in person, driving her and pushing her to the front.

It was almost eleven at night on Sunday. With yet another black coffee, she stared at her laptop. She needed a proper finishing sequence.

"Done?" the message beeped.

About to wind up, she replied, "Almost."

He replied with a heart emoticon.

Her heart fluttered as though it was virtual.

Was he attempting to tell her something?

'Don't read more into it, Ananya. He has always been this caring right from the beginning. Don't forget how you got hurt last time,' her mind cautioned sternly.

She replied with a smile. Pushing thoughts of Anshik aside, she completed the script to her satisfaction and emailed the marketing team.

Her mother's words strengthened her willpower and brought her back. Somewhere deep within, she believed that her life would change soon.

She dedicated her office hours to her job and spent her evenings at a nearby coffee shop, pursuing her passion with her laptop. Determined, she sought new ideas for her stories to pitch them to production houses.

After a week of scrutiny from the marketing team, she received an email that took her to a state of elation. They had selected her script for the advertisement.

In her cheerful mood, she overlooked Anshik, who had come to the cafeteria through the back door. Her eyes crinkled with contentment.

"Gosh . . . this is true," she muttered, pinching herself. "Ouch!"

It was hardly nine in the morning, and no one was around to watch her antics. People were yet to come. She hugged the laptop in delight, and pouting her lips, she kissed the screen.

"Lucky laptop," commented Anshik from behind.

Shocked, she turned to him.

"When did you come?"

"I came in when you were romancing your laptop."

Thinking of the email, she ran to him and hugged him. Her previous inhibitions were broken.

"My script is selected, Anshik," she informed him joyfully.

"Yeah, I saw the list and here I am to wish you."

"Thank you."

"Don't thank me. I did nothing. It is your flair for your passion that has got you selected. But remember, Ananya . . . you are on your first step."

"Yes, I know Anshik. But I feel excited and can't seem to control this rush of feeling."

"I can understand that with the way you are crushing me." He laughed.

Embarrassed, she moved away from him, letting him go out of her overbearing hug.

"Were you a part of the jury?"

He shook his head. "No, but Tanvi was a part of it. She is an IIM graduate in marketing and knows what works best."

"Hah, the gorgeous Tanvi," she murmured, her enthusiasm dwindling a little.

"Yeah, the beautiful friend of mine," he agreed.

"Whatever you say, I will not let you spoil my mood."

"I don't want to do that. Enjoy your first victory, Ananya. Many more to come," he wished her sincerely and passed her a gift box.

Astonished, she got it with a query in her eyes. "Open up," he ordered. Peeling away the layers of the wrapper, there was a handmade diary with an antique lock and key.

"This is beautiful, Ansh."

She did not notice the way she had addressed him, and it came out of her spontaneously.

"Keep filling this diary with your stories, Ananya. Lock it. When the right time comes, let the world see what you have got."

His words brought in tears, and she nodded speechlessly.

"And when you are shooting for the ad, I will relieve you of your duties at the cafeteria. Anil will assign someone else for the duration."

Ananya pinched herself. *'Are things happening for real?'*

*****

The past two weeks had gone on a hectic mode. She collaborated with the top technicians and learnt a lot, from camera angles to creating beautiful visuals on the screen. Anshik was there most of the time, and she ensured she was not distracted by him.

She had to deliver the best, for all their sakes. With that thought, she had put her heart and soul into her work, which showed in the output they had come up with.

It was the day of results. She walked inside Anshik's cubicle anxiously. Wearing a royal blue suit against a pale gray silk shirt, he looked like royalty, peering at his laptop. Her white T-shirt and blue jeans appeared casual against his dressing.

But the office culture promoted casual dressing among the employees. Probably, he was meeting some bigshot today. Her thoughts traversed in multiple directions. Their job was done yesterday, and he had called her the first thing this morning.

"Oh God, why is he frowning?"

"Anshik," she called, realizing his mind was miles away.

Turning to her voice, he asked her intently. "Do you want to know the verdict?"

He got up from his chair and went near her.

She put her hands against her ears and closed her eyes.

"I want to, but I am scared."

Moving closer, he removed her hands and whispered with his breath hot against her ears.

"When you have put in all your effort, why are you scared? Your heart is racing, Ananya. I can hear the beats outside."

"Anshik, please."

"Okay, I'll not hold the suspense. It is a tremendous success. It was posted by top influencers across social media, and it has become viral, Ananya."

"Really?" she whispered in awe.

He pulled her and showed her his laptop. "Look."

With millions of views in a day, it has connected with the right audience.

He opened his mailbox. "I have got multiple requests from the clients today."

"Congratulations, Ananya! You did it."

He lifted her high and swirled her around.

"Wah . . . Anshik, we are at the office." She laughed.

"And my door is closed."

"Put me down."

"Never down, Anu."

"I meant—"

"I know but you are on the right track."

"All thanks to you."

But her mind went wayward as her stomach was crushed against his chest. He brought her down gently, and their eyes locked. Her hands chained against his shoulders as her T-shirt touched his suit. With hardly any gap, she made the first move and brushed her lips against his forehead.

"What are you doing?" he asked, a little dazed.

"Thanking you."

With brimming contentment, she took his face in her hands.

"You don't have to . . . I did nothing."

"Don't you want me to kiss you?"

Stunned at her query, his eyes sought hers, reading her intent.

She stepped closer and covered his lips as her legs reached the floor.

A dizzying sensation ripped him at her touch, and his level of craving shot up. He desperately wanted to celebrate the moment and give in completely, but he knew that she was just on her first step. They had to stall their relationship until she reached a substantial position in her career.

'God, she is a temptation in disguise.'

Involuntarily, his hands tightened his hold around her. Her kiss was sensual, and soft, yet triggered his wild desire and burnt him. With her embrace, she took his strength and fed him an elixir along the way. They molded against each other with unspoken emotions overruling them.

Unable to control himself, he yanked her toward him and kissed her, taking the initiative in his hands and dominating her.

His mouth opened against her and tasted the ecstasy she shared. His fingers held her hips, strengthening their stance.

"Ansh," she muttered against his throat.

That brought him back to his senses, and he pulled back consciously.

She looked at him, confused, as he moved back to his chair. Then he spoke as if nothing earth-shattering had happened a few seconds prior.

"We have organized a party at the office in the evening to celebrate this success. I came here to invite my employee, who has done her best."

His last words underlined that she was just an employee, and what they had shared earlier was nothing to him. With mounting anger, she shouted back at him.

"Thanks, Mr. Anshik Dhawan. I'll be there. It is magnanimous on the head of the company to invite a paltry employee like me, definitely not by kissing me."

Anshik wanted to explain, but she cut him short as she raised her hands to halt him. "I will meet you at six today. Please go."

*****

Fuming with anger, she went to her hostel and picked up a dress for the evening party and came back. She was sure that Anshik had feelings for her, but why did he behave oddly? Each time they kissed, she sensed their soul connection. Could he not see that?

She knew that he could not see her hurt or down. Then why did he not acknowledge what he was feeling? And to top it, he makes sure that he covers up his care for her as if it is all official concern, and Ananya knew it was not the case.

'*Watch out, Mr. Anshik Dhawan. Let me make you reveal what you feel for me today.*'

Though she felt positive about her approach, an element of doubt crept inside. Would history repeat itself? Would he conclude all they shared was a long-term friendship?

It was 5.30 p.m.

Taking all her items to change, she went to the restroom to get ready. She wore a short, sleeveless silk red dress, tied her hair up in a messy bun, wore a dash of scarlet red lipstick, and lined her eyes with dark eyeliner.

Her apple-like cheeks glowed with a touch of a natural-shade blush. With long ear hoops and pointed heels, she was all set for the office party. Happy with her efforts, she knew she looked great.

'*Here, I come, Anshik. You will speak the truth today.*'

As she returned to her desk to pick up her handbag, Anil whistled.

"Wow, Ananya . . . you are dazzling."

Gagan, her teammate, agreed. "Agree, Mr. Anil. Ananya looks pretty today."

"Ananya looks pretty on all days," he retorted.

Her confidence went up a notch. '*Watch out, Anshik . . .*' she spoke inside.

Turning back to Anil, she looped her hands in his arms and asked, "You look great yourself. Shall we go?"

"My pleasure, Ananya." Anil was happy that Ananya had noted that he had changed into a yellow party shirt.

Gagan and Vaishnavi told them they would join them in another ten minutes. "Guys, you go ahead," they said.

"Make it faster," commanded Anil as he and Ananya went to the office auditorium.

Anshik noted her the moment she stepped inside the auditorium. He was seated along with Tanvi and the marketing team on the stage. He could not take her eyes from her stunning look and controlled his urge to drag her out of Anil's hold.

His possessiveness erupted out of nowhere, and he wanted to rip the eyes of men who had their eyes on her.

And he caught her glance. As if she could read his thoughts, she whispered, "Try it . . ."

'Little witch. I can read your intentions. But I will not react the way you want. Behave.'

They conversed in their own world.

Ananya took her place with Anil by her side.

'Calm down.' Anshik self-instructed. He had a speech to deliver and present the trophies to the advertising team.

Ananya gave up her hope. She knew from his reaction that Anshik would not react. He had built a barrier around his feelings and had to break that himself. That thought pulled her down miserably.

Anil shook her. "Go."

Only then did she realize her name was read out, and she needed to go to the stage. She climbed to the dais and quickly got the shield without glancing at him.

When the presenter prompted her to talk, she thanked everyone on her team and came down.

"I'll leave," she whispered to Anil.

"What is wrong? Don't you want to stay? This is your day. Why don't you enjoy that? Look at the delightful food over there. That is for us. At least eat and go. I can imagine what dinner awaits you at your hostel."

Anil was right. Thinking of the food at her hostel made

her stomach curdle. She had to finish her dinner. The event was also done.

Piling her plate with food, she looked around to see Anshik doing the same. She saw people standing in groups, enjoying the buffet. She heard laughter and conversation here and there as she walked through the crowd.

"Communication is the key . . ." someone seemed to give relationship advice. Ananya acknowledged the thought.

Should she let him know what she felt about him? Should she tell him that her heart flutters when he comes close and cries when he is not with her?

She walked to him, determined. He turned to the other side but did not see her.

Nearing him, she realized he was talking with someone else. Peering, she noted it was Tanvi, and their voices were whispering.

"Tanvi."

"Ansh, it was always love for you that prompted me to do things which I would not do for anyone else in this world. I initially thought Ananya was your dream girl, and I should not step on your toes. But when I worked with both of you on this advertisement, I realized that is not the case. You guys hardly spoke with each other, and I thought I still had a chance with you. We talk together . . . laugh together . . . work together . . . why don't we start our life as a couple?"

Ananya turned to Anshik. His eyes spoke a lot of emotions. With a heavy heart, she walked away from them. She would not listen to him confessing his love for another female.

She knew that she would fall apart if she stayed there for a second longer. Setting aside the plate, she ran outside crazily, but the cold Pune breeze did not calm her feelings that ripped her insides.

Her running had brought her to the rooftop coffee shop, where she used to write frequently. She slumped into a seat in the corner, feeling dejected over the recent event. She turned and saw couples holding hands, sharing coffee, under the night sky with a candle on the table.

A sigh escaped her.

'This would never happen in her life.'

That thought broke her, and she cried uncontrollably. The server prompted her, "Are you okay? What do you want, ma'am?"

Wiping her tears away, she snatched the menu card from him, and the menu appeared hazy to her. She pointed randomly to something.

"Are you sure?" questioned the bearer.

"Yes, please."

The server nodded with a frown. She was in unbearable sorrow, and this would help.

He brought in a brown liquid, which was neither hot nor too cold. But it had the smell of coffee.

Ananya took a sip and found that it was bitter. But she liked the taste.

She gulped down the contents until it was empty. She showed it to the server that she wanted one more.

In a few minutes, she felt light-headed. She took out her mobile and called him.

"Mr. Anshik Dhawan." Her voice was slurred.

"Ananya." He sounded alert.

"Congratulations, sir!"

"Where are you?"

"Where am I?" She looked around, shivering a little.

"Out, boss. I am celebrating for you," she declared.

"Are you drinking, Ananya?" he asked her with a doubt.

"Drinking? Why should I? I am just having my coffee."

The server came and kept another glass in front of her.

"Here you go. One more coffee shot for you."

"Oh God, you are having coffee shots, not coffee."

"What difference does that make?"

He didn't want to argue with her, so he asked, "Where are you?"

"Why should I tell you? You need not take care of me. You have Tanvi to look after."

Anshik fisted his hand in anger. "Don't be a fool, Ananya."

"Fool? Yeah, I might be for believing you."

"Just tell me where you are," he threatened.

A girl crossed her, talking over the phone to her boyfriend. "I came to the rooftop coffee shop, dear. Come soon."

Ananya glared at the back of the unknown lady. *'Why is fate playing against me today?'*

Listening to that vital information, Anshik rushed to the spot. It was hardly five minutes from his office.

Finishing the second shot the server had brought in, she staggered a little as she tried to stand.

"Ananya . . ." Anshik went to her and caught hold of her hands, steadying her.

She pushed him away and asked, "What are you doing here?"

"I could ask the same of you."

He still did not let go of her.

"Go to your new fiancée, Tanvi." She pushed him back.

"Were you eavesdropping on my conversation, Ananya?"

"I did not. I just came to tell you about my—"

"About your?" he prompted her as she paused.

186

"It does not matter now."

"Yes, nothing matters, and I'll take you to your place."

"No, I want another cup of coffee," she demanded.

"NO. On second thought, I'll take you to my home today. You had coffee shots."

"Yeah, they were great," she declared.

"It is vodka mixed with coffee!"

"Oh, does that mean I had alcohol now?" She was astonished.

"Yes. And you are in no fit state to stay alone."

"But I can't come with you," she denied, shaking her head.

"You have come often to my home. What is the difference?"

"Tanvi will get this wrong."

"No, she would not. My mother is at home. So you are safely chaperoned," he told her.

She tried pushing him away, but he seemed immovable. "No."

"Yes, Ananya. You are coming with me. That is final."

She was not in a state to argue. Holding her, he took her to his car. Taking the front seat, she realized that Anshik had not denied anything that she spoke about Tanvi, which meant that he had agreed to her proposal.

The atmosphere inside the car was gloomy, and it took another ten minutes to reach his home. He honked his car, but his door security was nowhere in sight.

He switched off the ignition at the main entrance.

"Oh gosh!" she exclaimed suddenly.

"What?"

"Why did you do everything for me?" she demanded, holding the collar of his shirt.

"I did not . . ."

"Stop denying, Anshik . . . at each step of my broken phase, you were with me . . . you still are . . ."

He turned to the other side, unable to answer her. What she said was true. His heart pained at her words.

'Hold on for some more time, Ananya . . . the moment I feel that you have reached what you had aimed for, I'll talk about my genuine feelings for you.'

Ananya continued, unaware of his internal thoughts.

"And when I try to understand what you feel for me, you deny everything . . ."

"You can't equate what I did for you to love . . ." he unconvincingly denied.

"If that is not love, I don't understand what love is," she came back fiercely.

He did not answer.

"Why did you kiss me then? And don't you dare to demean our intimacy like last time . . . I'll not believe you." She screamed with her emotions threatening to explode, and she hugged him hard.

"Please . . . don't do this to us again, Ansh . . ."

"Ananya . . . you don't know what you are talking about."

"Then tell me . . . why are you denying our relationship?"

He was silent, and that silence brought her to senses.

"Sorry . . ." she stopped, remembering that Tanvi was waiting for him. Brushing her tears, she moved away.

"Where has your security gone?"

"I'll check," volunteered Anshik as he got out of his car.

Feeling suffocated, Ananya also stepped out. Turning to the other side, she saw a small ice-cream vendor on the other side of the road.

Intoxication took over her sorrow. "Probably, ice-cream could cure my pain," she whispered dramatically.

Peering through the gap in the gate, Anshik tried to call his security.

She staggered a little. Holding the door, she tried to stand tall and walked across the road toward the caravan. Anshik turned to see her. A speeding car cruised toward her.

"Ananya!"

Her sluggish brain processed what was happening as she froze in the middle.

"No." He ran to her. But it was too late.

Hit by the car, she was thrown away, and she rolled on the road.

"Ananya!" he screamed as she fell at his feet. Blood oozed out of her head.

CHAPTER 18

The Success Story

*Once you restart the journey of your life after a
breakdown, don't stop ever. There might be miles
to cover, but with each uncertain step you take, you
are nearing your destination with that step.*

Carrying Ananya in his hands, Anshik quickly
but carefully placed her on the backseat
of his car. She was unconscious, with
blood spurting out from the back of her head. The
hospital was nearby, and he did not want to wait for
the ambulance. The moment he started his car, the
thought of losing her frightened him to the core.
Should he have been vocal about his feelings?

"God, Ananya. Can't you understand what I
feel for you?"

Her body shuddered.

'Please, God . . . let Ananya be safe. The world
is nothing without her . . .'

He let out a frustrated sigh and muttered, "Ananya, I tell you about my feelings in all ways. My kisses, my touch, the possessiveness that peeps out whenever you are around . . . everything tells you what I feel for you."

"I can't live without you and in your heart, you know that well."

His pathetic monologue continued.

"Three years without you was hell. And I can't even imagine a day without you anymore."

Pain speared his heart, and his body trembled at the thought of a life without her. Hitting his hand against the car steering, he whispered, "God, if something has to happen, let me be the recipient. Please let her live."

He parked the car at the emergency entrance and rushed inside. The attendants swiftly brought the stretcher and took her in carefully. It was almost eleven at night.

The duty doctor took her in for an examination. An hour passed by. To Anshik, it felt like days. He called his mother and informed her about Ananya.

"Take care of her, *beta*. And bring her here when she is okay," she said.

Anshik peered inside, waiting for the doctor to come out. Another half an hour went by. His legs hurt with all his walking across the hospital floor, worrying about her.

The door opened, and the doctor walked out. Breathlessly, he waited for him to pronounce the verdict.

"Don't worry, Mr. Dhawan. Your friend is stronger than you think. She is alright. The blood that came from the back of her head was from a cut by a sharp object on the road when she fell. The injuries she has are external. I have taken a CT scan for confirmation. No threatening internal injuries or clots."

Anshik felt relieved.

"She was unconscious because she had lost blood."

"Is she okay now?"

"Yes, she is, except for the fracture in her right hand."

"Oh, is it?" he asked worriedly.

"Yes, she had fallen on her right hand. It is minor and might take a month to heal. I have bandaged her hand and arm to keep it immobile."

"Can we leave then?"

"I have administered a bottle of drip. Once it is done, you can take her. Monitor her, though, just in case. And if you observe anything abnormal, bring her here immediately."

"Thank you so much, doctor." He gripped his hand in gratitude. To him, the doctor appeared as a God in disguise.

"Relax, Mr. Dhawan. Things are fine. All she needs is rest."

He nodded and rushed in to meet her.

"Ananya," he called.

Her eyes were wide open, and she had a small bandage on her forehead and backside. They had completely wrapped her right hand into a white caster. She tried to get up as she noticed him.

"Ah." The needle on her other hand pricked.

"Lie back. Don't strain."

"You gave me quite a scare, Ananya. Why did you have to cross the road? You were intoxicated!"

"No."

"Don't you get it? I told you earlier. You did not have coffee; they were coffee shots—coffee mixed with vodka."

She gasped. "Oh, I just wanted to have some ice-cream."

He sighed.

"I'll get you many. But never try these stunts in the future."

"It was not intentional." She pouted.

"I know, and hence it is scarier," he warned sternly.

She searched for her watch with one hand completely plastered and the other injected with a cannula connected to a drip bottle.

"If you want to know the time, it is two in the night."

She gasped. "My hostel would be closed by now."

"Who said you are going back to your hostel?"

"But, Anshik—"

"No arguments, Ananya. You are coming with me, and that is final."

"What would your parents say?"

"My mother was the one who invited you. You can use Kavya's room."

She faltered. "I don't want to trouble you anymore."

"Believe it or not, you have troubled me from day one."

She turned to look for a pillow to throw at him.

"You know, you can't." He laughed.

Coming near, he murmured, "I agree that you are my trouble but I can't live without this trouble."

At that moment, she felt she had everything in this world. The nurse walked in and removed the needle from her hands.

Giving Ananya the medicines and a prescription sheet, she said, "Give her the medicines without fail. Come back after a week. We will have to change her dressing."

"Can I leave?" Ananya asked the nurse, not wanting to extend her hospital time.

"Yes, definitely."

*****

194

Ananya woke up the next day in Kavya's room. Mrs. Dhawan held a plate of steaming *dosa*, and Anshik was sleeping on a sofa near her. Her voice alerted him, and he woke up.

"Are you alright?" he demanded.

She nodded.

"He has gone crazy, Ananya. He did not want to leave you unattended even for a second."

She blushed and bent her head a little, avoiding their gazes.

"I would have done the same for Kavya," he retaliated.

"Oh, does that mean you consider Ananya as your sister?"

"NO."

"He considers me as his friend, aunty and he would do anything for his friends," she retorted sarcastically.

"Friend? Is that what he told you?" Sheela put her hands on her hips.

"Don't perform a post-mortem of my feelings," he cut both of them sternly and got the plate from his mother.

"I will take care of Ananya," he informed.

His mother laughed and left the room.

Reading his intention, she said, "That is okay, Anshik. I'll eat on my own."

"Will you eat *dosa* with a spoon? I don't see any other alternative."

She felt awkward in her hospital gown. Though he was sleepy, Anshik appeared gorgeous in his gray pajamas.

"We have office today," she reminded him.

"Don't think of coming to the office until you are perfectly alright. And I have already taken a week off."

"What?" She gasped.

"I can't just leave you all alone in this state." His voice was firm, brooking no argument.

"Why should you take care of me?"

They stared at each other, getting into a deadlock scenario.

"Let us not talk about it now. I informed your brother about your accident yesterday, and he was genuinely worried about you. I promised him that I'll take care of you. He wants to meet you, Anu, but I could sense his guilt because of his past behavior toward you. Your mother's letter has not only changed you, but Sandeep too. He would definitely call you."

The heaviness in her heart seemed to fade away. Things were getting better.

"Now be a good girl and open your mouth."

He dipped a piece of dosa in coconut chutney and fed her.

Ananya had an uncontrollable urge to hug him and thank him for taking care of her, but there was still an invisible barrier that he had forcefully erupted between them.

Glad that she had completed her breakfast, he got up.

"Take rest. That is what the doctor has advised for you."

"No."

He stared at her. "I did not ask you a question, Ananya."

"I can't afford to rest the entire day."

Anshik blinked in confusion. "Why?"

"Ansh, I wanted to tell you this yesterday. Your diary is working like a lucky charm for me."

He lifted his eyebrows in a query.

"I submitted my idea for an OTT series with *JetFlix* and they are interested in taking it up further."

A wave of delight passed through his eyes.

At last, everything was coming together.

"Happy for you, Ananya."

"I know you would be. Resting isn't an option for me right

now, as you now know. The story line was submitted. But I have to give them the entire script by this week."

"Your health is more important than any opportunity," he chided.

"I can't give up, Ansh. It would not be the right thing to do. I can't give up on my first hurdle."

Seeing the fighting spirit in her eyes, Anshik left the room silently.

She was disappointed. But he came back within a couple of minutes.

Dragging a wooden chair near her, he sat with a laptop in his hands. She looked at him, confused.

"What are you doing?"

"I'll be your hand."

"What?"

"Can't you hear me?"

"I can. Have you gone crazy?" she demanded.

"Ha ha. I told you I'll be your right hand. You have the story line and I'll write the script for you. You do the narration."

She was stunned at his gesture. "Do you want to do this?"

"Of course."

Touched by his care for her, she dabbed his cheeks. "Thank you, Ansh but it is not a straightforward task."

"I run a corporate company, Ananya."

"That is different and this is something else. But I am pleased that you want to help me."

"I don't think it is. You will narrate and I am just going to help you by either writing it on a paper or typing on my laptop."

"Sometimes, I struggle to create a scene. On other days, I can't stop at all. It is time-consuming."

"Do not worry about my time, Ananya. Think about you."

She held his hands, wondering how he could be so giving. Despite that, he maintains that she is just a friend. She sighed as her heart dipped at that thought.

"Take some rest. I will assist you with your script this week."

*****

True to his words, Anshik helped her to get her script ready. Sometimes, she narrated the script the entire night. And he captured everything in his laptop and never showed a sign of tiredness. He was ensnared by her and her writing. With her right hand still held by the cast, he fed her all three times a day.

In her entire life, Ananya felt as if she was never pampered this way. The next week, he took her to the hospital, and they changed her cast and redid the dressing.

She held his hand as he was about to feed her chapati for dinner.

"Ansh." She was in tears, moved by his affection.

Her voice triggered his curiosity.

"Thank you."

"*Arre*, stuff your thanks into the dustbin, Ananya. I don't want it. I do this because I want to."

"No one has ever taken care of me like this before."

She sat on the cot, and he held her tenderly.

"Don't be emotional. Put this into your scripts."

"I don't want to ask anything further or take advantage of our friendship. But I need two months off," she told him.

"I have told you already. Until and unless you are completely alright, I'll not permit you inside the office."

"I am not asking for the leaves for my recovery."

"Then?"

"Come closer." She pointed at her mobile.

"With pleasure." He smiled and peered into the screen to see an email congratulating her.

"Wow, *JetFlix* accepted your script?"

She nodded with gratitude, and he hugged her with delight.

They shed tears of joy, enjoying the preciousness of the moment.

"This is a big break for you, Anu."

"I know."

"You don't require a job at my office anymore."

"I don't know. They have asked me to report to *DreamStudios* from tomorrow, and the shoot is scheduled for two months."

"Go ahead, Ananya. Don't worry about the office. I'll manage. That is the advantage of being the boss."

She kissed his forehead gently. A vision of Tanvi flashed before her, and she moved back as if someone had slapped her. He had not yet given her clarity on his relationship with Tanvi. But she had not seen her since her accident.

Anshik was with her the entire day, and she had not seen him calling her, not even once. Why was he keeping her in the dark about his relationship with Tanvi? She had attempted to ask about her twice, and he had evaded her questions deliberately.

"Ahem . . ."

There was a noise from the door.

"May I know the reason for your celebration? I see tears of happiness all around. Come on, tell me." Mrs. Dhawan walked in with a cup of *kheer*.

"Wow, ma. You brought us sweets at the right time. You will soon be able to see Ananya's story on *JetFlix*."

"Congratulations, dear!" The elderly lady gave her a hug, and the trio ate the kheer happily.

"By the way, did your brother call you, Ananya?" Anshik asked.

"He did not, but he sent a message though, wishing me good health."

"He will come around, don't worry."

His mobile rang. Anshik exited the room to take the call. Mrs. Dhawan turned to her. "We are all happy for you, Ananya. You deserve this success. I know you were the driving force behind my son's career. And this is the best we could do to repay you."

"Aunty, please, I am embarrassed."

"Embarrassed? Outsiders feel so. I don't want you to feel that way. And remember that you are always one amongst us, Ananya. I'll be delighted to welcome you to our house any time."

With a hidden, cryptic note between her words for her to decode, Mrs. Dhawan left to water her garden.

'What do I tell you, aunty? I agree that Anshik helps and cares for me. But not as my love, but as my friend. Despite asking him many times, he has always done his best to deny our relationship. I am not sure of the equation that he shares with Tanvi, either. I am upset and hurt beyond words. And I am tuning my mind to accept his decision.'

Her heart spoke the truth.

Anshik came back after completing his call.

"All geared up, Ananya?" he asked.

She nodded enthusiastically, hiding her pain, but he appeared doubly pleased for her.

"I don't know if you were waiting for your break, Ananya but I was. We can soon . . ." He paused.

"Soon?"

He shook his head. "Pull this off successfully, and then I'll tell you."

"Alright," she accepted grudgingly.

Seeing her disappointed face, he caught the tip of her nose and pinched it a little. "I'll tell you for sure. But you need to put all your efforts on the Himalayan task in front of you."

"Aye, aye, sir."

*****

Neither Anshik nor Ananya knew how the next couple of months went. Anshik dropped her at the studio early in the morning and picked her up when the team had packed up for the day—sometimes in the evenings or late nights.

The Dhawan family could have sent her food through any of their servants, but Anshik brought it regularly and fed her until they removed the cast from her hands.

"I don't think I could have tackled this sick phase of mine without you," she told him.

He covered her lips with his fingers.

"I don't think so. You would have done it either way, with or without my support. I saw the fighting spirit back in your eyes when you agreed to live again. You would not have failed, Ananya."

She was tempted to run to him as if he was her lifeline.

"Thanks."

"Not again."

"I mean it."

"Are you not going to the studio today?" he changed the track of the conversation, not interested in her gratitude.

"It is all done. We have wrapped up the quick series," she told him proudly.

"Really? All our problems are sorted out then," concluded Anshik happily.

"Is it? I don't think so. I still have to pay my hostel fees, as I have not vacated. It has been pending for quite some time, and I have received the first payment for my series."

"I have paid for it already, Ananya."

"Oh, that is why they did not call me. I'll pay you then. I can't be in debt."

Her words irritated him, yet he controlled his anger.

"You can do it after we visit the temple."

"The Broken Trishul temple?"

"Where else? That is where everything started."

"You are right."

"I am always right, Miss Mehta."

She put her tongue outside, teasing him.

Anshik smiled at her gesture. She looked adorable in her blue cotton sari. It was not grand, yet she projected an elegance that can never be imitated. Lining her eyes darkly, she had applied pink gloss on her lips, and this weird combo tempted him badly.

"You are looking like an adorable monkey." He laughed outright.

"I'll bite you, Mr. Dhawan. Just because you are handsome with a magnificent physique does not mean you can call me a monkey," she threatened.

Wearing a collared yellow full-hand shirt with black pants, he looked his best.

"Point one—I did not call you monkey. I termed you as an adorable monkey, and two—do I look handsome to you?"

She gasped. She had not meant to blurt it unexpectedly.

"And three—you can bite. I promise I won't make noise."

"If I am an adorable monkey, you are a handsome devil."

His eyes became intense. She was not sure how it suddenly became sensual in a light-teasing atmosphere. They stood there, gaping at each other, not comprehending the magnetic pull that they shared.

"Anshik, you told me we could go to the temple," she reminded him, to halt the moment.

"Yes, we must. I have something important to tell you."

"Same here." They smiled together.

*****

They stood at the temple, praying, and thanking Mahadev from their heart. Turning, Ananya took an invitation from her handbag and passed it to him.

With a questioning look, he read the invite.

Dream Studios invites you to join us for the launch and teaser show of our new OTT series—ONE DAY, LIFE WILL CHANGE. If you are interested in watching the rest of the series, please watch it on JetFlix in the future!

Venue: Hotel Starz
Chief Guest:
Mr. Anshik Dhawan, CEO,
TechWarriors

He was dumbfounded. He had never expected this kind of honor when she had told him that she had something to share with him.

"Ansh, this is what we promised here . . . that you would be a CEO someday and I would invite you for my show. Would you do the honor of being the chief guest?"

He nodded with pride.

"And, Ansh, I have an important meeting with a top producer tomorrow. If all goes okay, you can watch another TV series of mine on Moon TV. If I can persuade him, the team might give me the prime slot at eight in the night."

They hugged and stood silently with smiles on their faces, enjoying their success together. There were tears in their eyes.

"How many hurdles we had gone through?"

She thought about her misfortunes and the bad phases she had experienced.

"Yeah, Ansh. But I feel it is all worth it in the end."

"That is my girl. But never cry."

He wiped her tears.

"*Arre*, Mr. Dhawan. These are tears of success."

'*What else are you waiting for, Anshik? Tell her. Enough of keeping her at one arm's distance. Tell her what you feel. Tell her that this is what love is—sharing the joy of success together.*'

Anshik put his hands inside his pocket and took out the diamond ring he had bought long back.

Ananya's mobile shrilled at the same time.

She looked at the screen.

"Oh God, Ansh. My papa is calling me."

She was excited. She told Anshik, "He has never called me . . . not once after I left home."

Keeping his ring inside, he put his hands on her shoulders. "Go ahead. Pick it up."

"Hello, papa . . ." Her hands trembled.

There was silence from the other end. Her father's voice was gruff.

"I heard of your web series from your brother. Congratulations, *beti*." His voice trembled as he wished her.

"Thanks, papa," she muttered tearfully.

"I apologize. I did not know what you had to go through, and my thinking was one-dimensional.

Not wanting to see her father in a weak, emotional state, she stopped him. "That is okay, papa."

"With all your dreams fulfilled now, will you come home, Ananya?"

"Yes, papa."

She responded immediately, as her heart had longed for that invitation from her father. "And I have a gift for you, Ananya."

"What is that, papa?"

"Do you remember Rahul?"

"Rahul?"

"Yes, the guy we fixed up for you before you left home. He is still waiting for you."

She gasped and turned to Anshik.

"I am waiting for you, *beti*. Will you come home today and mend fences with me?"

Thinking that her father had a change of heart, Anshik whispered, "If your father is calling you home, don't delay. Go ahead."

She nodded. "I'll come home, papa."

CHAPTER 19

The Separation

Separation pains and living with distress is difficult. But your mental strength can overcome this hurdle of agony.

Anshik missed Ananya crazily for the past two days. He could not wait any longer. Each second became unbearable. His feelings for her threatened to overflow, and the dam he had constructed against his emotions cracked. He wanted to pour his feelings into her. Though he could not blame her, he wanted to scream at her for doubting his love all these days. It was time to come clean, and there was no reason to hide behind the smoke screen.

He could have called her and asked about her visit, but he did not want to be overbearing. Giving her the personal space to heal the rift with her father, he did not disturb her. Things were getting back on track, and he knew how much she longed for a good bond with her father.

The calling bell rang. It was 11.00 a.m. on Sunday.

He ran to the porch.

"Relax, Anshik. She will not run away," his mother teased.

With a half-smile on his lips, he opened the door.

In a yellow and violet interleaved salwar, she looked striking. Her hair was braided into a *French-knot,* and she wore a pair of white studs. She carried out the traditional attire with grace.

Mrs. Dhawan saw her son with eyes full of love. In his casual gray shirt and ivory pants, he was good-looking, and standing near each other, they made a perfect couple. She wished they would get together soon.

"You are early," Anshik commented the moment he saw her. His body language spoke of excitement, which he tried hard to hide.

"Yeah." Her reply was non-committal.

Something was odd, and she was not ready to meet his eyes.

"Ananya, is something wrong?" he asked with concern.

"No . . ." she faltered.

"All issues with your father sorted? Is he on your side?"

"Yes."

"Is he happy now?"

"More than happy."

There was a whimper in her voice. She clasped her bag tightly.

"Give me your bag."

He took her bag, and their fingers brushed.

Cling. Her ring fell.

"Gift from your father?" he asked as he picked up but stopped in between. A sparkling white stone sat grandly on its golden heart.

"Who gave you this?" His tone had altered.

Shocked, his query was almost inaudible, but to Ananya, it was as if he shouted from the top of the building.

She stepped inside, avoiding confrontation, not wanting to create a scene outside. She would have gone past him if he had not dragged her and held her tight.

"Who gave this to you?" he reiterated.

His stern voice brought his mother to the living room.

"Rahul," she whispered, doubting her decision noting Anshik's reaction.

Her only intention had been to keep her father happy by respecting his wish, and she was sure that her decision would not affect Anshik, as he had claimed multiple times that she was just his friend.

Her only trouble was she did not know how she would throw away the powerful, over-consuming love which she had for him and move on.

"Ananya!" he screamed in rage.

'Has she miscalculated my feelings?'

Calming himself, he asked, "Who is Rahul? I have never heard of him."

"He was the one with whom my marriage was fixed before I left home."

She paused momentarily and realized that Anshik and his mother expected her to elaborate.

"Though the engagement was called off, he had waited for me for all these years. This trait impressed my father, and he told me that there couldn't be a better match for me than Rahul. And once I went back."

"Your father got you engaged to that saintly Rahul again. *Wah* . . . and you did not speak a word against it?"

He clapped his hands in a sarcastic applause and looked at her in disbelief. Believing they needed privacy to sort out this misunderstanding, his mother went inside.

Prior to that, she warned her son, "Stay calm, *beta*. Anger will spoil everything."

Ignoring her warning, he turned to Ananya and pulled her close, clutching her hands.

"It hurts, Ansh," she pleaded, trying to escape his hold.

As if he were burnt, he pushed her away.

"And you said okay?"

His gaze speared into hers.

"What else can I do?"

His eyes demanded silently—'*Does our relationship mean nothing to you?*'

Ananya tried her best to read his intention behind the veil of anger.

He lifted his eyebrows in desperation and let out a frustrated sigh. Things were beyond his control.

He held her by her shoulders. Before he could bombard her with the following question, she volunteered, "I wanted to make my father happy, Anshik. I thought you would understand me."

He stepped back as if she was talking to him in an alien language.

"You come back to me after getting engaged to some random guy and you expect me to support you?"

"You are my friend, and you are supposed to be happy for

me," she argued, not understanding the depth of his feelings for her.

"Now I get it. You are in a revenge mode. You are getting back at me for what happened between us years ago."

"No," she cried.

"What else?" His voice was emotional. He threw the vase, kept on the corner table. The glass shattered along the floor.

She closed her ears.

"Stop this, Ansh." She held his hands.

He threw her hands away from him.

His anger hurt her mentally, and she wanted to sit back in a corner and cry.

"Why should it matter to you?"

Her query cruised through him like a bullet. But words of love stuck in his throat. How could he propose to an engaged woman?

With tear-glazed eyes, she continued her emotional tirade. "You kept repeating till last week that we share nothing but a beautiful bond of friendship."

His eyes were wet with agony. Could she not read his heart then?

"So all that mattered to you were words, right? Could you not sense the connection that tied our souls, no matter how hard we tried to break it?"

"What do you mean, Ansh?" She held his collar, despite his rejection.

"Nothing."

He tugged her hands away. Getting a grip of his emotions momentarily, he continued, "I get it, Ananya. If your decision makes you happy, go ahead. Who am I to stop you?"

With those dismal words, he stomped to his room on the first floor. Utterly confused with his attitude, she ran after him as her heart pained to see him hurt and angry.

But before she could reach him, he took his bike keys from his room and stormed out.

"Anshik!" she cried. But without heeding her, he went out. Ananya wanted to run to him, like she had done years earlier, but he was too agile for her. He had already left. She sighed miserably.

What was she going to do?

His room was partly open. Usually, he kept his personal space closed, and she had gone in twice, only when he was there.

Something prompted her to step into his room. There was a notebook on the table, which fluttered with the air from the balcony. She ran and picked it up but found it empty. Disappointed, she was about to close when she saw her face sketched skillfully as a portrait. It was beautiful, but what stunned her was the line underneath the drawing.

'*Waiting for you to be mine forever—Anshik.*'

"Oh gosh . . ."

Was she mistaken about his feelings?

'*Why did he then kept repeating that she was his friend?*'

She knew what she was doing was wrong, but she wanted to explore his room and get her answers once and for all. There was a half-opened box, and she picked it up. It had the gifts that they had shared earlier.

Along with those precious memories, there was a diary, obscured by the other items in the box. The bell gonged somewhere. It was twelve in the noon. She gazed out of the balcony.

To her disappointment, instead of being sunny and breezy, it had become cloudy suddenly. The dark skies shook with thunder. The ripping sound made her almost deaf, and it took her a couple of seconds to recover.

'*Where did Anshik go?*'

She was worried about him and was sure it would rain cats and dogs. Her attention came back to the diary in her hand. She flipped through the pages and realized that he had penned down every incident that took place between them.

A folded sheet of paper fell out, and she cried as she read its content.

Dear Ananya,

Years ago, I let you go. I had to. I had no other choice. My father was on his deathbed with his suicide attempt, which was a pathetic idea to support my dreams, though his intention was good.

After that, my responsibilities doubled, and I had to fulfil my duty as a son. I had to earn the money for his operation that he desperately needed. I had no means of supporting you at that point, with no career of my own. Without money to support you or my family, I felt it was wrong on my part to hold you. I had dreams to chase, and I had to let you go. I let you fly away. Do you know how hard it was for me?

I did the unthinkable! It still pains me to think of the day we parted. I lost myself completely. I cannot count the number of sleepless nights or the nightmares I have had ever since you left. Our separation became a mental illness for me. It made me sick and brought tears into my eyes whenever I was reminded of you. The worst part was each and everything in my life made me think of you.

It was tough, and the phase was cruel. But the thought that if I succeed in life, I can come back to claim you pushed me, inspired me to move mountains. And I prayed that you would wait for me.

I fought all my personal demons to succeed in my dreams. I fueled my passion with the pain. That helped. After I became successful, I wanted to meet you desperately, and I was gifted with a God-sent opportunity. From that moment, I never wanted to let go of you for even a second.

But this time, you had built an invisible barrier around you. You were broken. I did not see the enthusiastic girl whom I had met years ago. I understood that you were scared of falling for me again. You were hurt. The rough patches that you have gone through had taken your dreams. I had to bring them back. And despite my love, whenever we were together, I promised myself that I would stay within my boundaries to help you. It was hard to follow the hands-off policy, though I violated it several times. Do you know how often I have wanted to tell you that I love you? But I knew I had to wait. Yet I made sure that I communicated my love to you in all other ways except words, hoping you would understand my feelings. I touched you . . . kissed you . . . hugged you . . . I was jealous like hell whenever you had Anil near you. I thought, with my actions, you would come to realize our special connection.

With your recent OTT series, you have started your dream career. I don't want to wait any longer. When will you come back, my dear Ananya? I want to scream my love for you. At the temple that day, I was on the verge of proposing to you. But you got the call from your father. And I thought I would wait. Hence, I am penning down this letter, venting out my feelings for you here. If not for your call, I would have told *you everything that day. You get your problems sorted out with your father, but come back to me, Anu. I am waiting for you as always. We have dreamt together, and now it is time for us to fly together . . .*

Ananya dropped onto the nearby bed with a thud.

"Instead of confusing me, you could have opened up to me. If you had asked me to wait, I would have. Why did you push me away? I loved you truly," she wailed against the paper as if the inanimate object could reply.

"How many times did I ask you about our relationship?" she whispered into thin air, hitting the pillow in desperation.

It thundered again. That made her jump anxiously. She peeped out of the big window and shuddered, as she was scared for Anshik. It began raining, and the sky was almost dark. The birds chirped at an ungodly hour, and the leaves fluttered with the cold air. The entire atmosphere gave her a depressing feeling.

"Where did you go? You still need to answer a few questions. You can't run away from me just like that!"

She spoke on her own and took her mobile out to call him.

It kept ringing, but he did not pick.

The door opened, and Mrs. Dhawan walked in.

"Where did he go?" she asked.

"I don't know, aunty. He took his bike keys and stormed out." Her voice went down with guilt, not realizing that the other woman was feeling guiltier than her.

Mrs. Dhawan held her forehead and sat down on the bed.

"Do you know, Ananya? I am responsible for all this chaos."

Ananya frowned in confusion.

"I knew. He would not have told you. He would never put me down."

She shook her head and confessed, "I asked him to let you go, Anu. I made him promise when his father was in deathbed. I did not mean to break you apart. All I wanted was to ensure that Anshik succeeded in his mission with no distractions. I am sorry. I thought I was doing something good for my son."

She held Ananya's hands and cried. "He loves you, Ananya. Don't let him go. I made the mistake, and he should not suffer for the same."

The mother was worried about her son, repenting her mistake.

Ananya cried in pain and hugged her. "I have always loved him, aunty. I just did not realize that he loves me back."

Mrs. Dhawan looked at her as if she had gone mad.

"He loved you ever since Kavya brought you home."

She looked at her in wonder. "Everyone knew . . ."

They had to bring Anshik back home.

Mrs. Dhawan dialed his number in vain. No reply from his end.

"Don't worry, aunty. I'll go out and look for him."

"It is not safe, dear," Sheela warned.

"I don't care, aunty. I can't sit inside twiddling my thumbs when I know Anshik is out there, suffering somewhere."

Taking Kavya's two-wheeler, Ananya went out.

Mrs. Dhawan had asked her to wear a raincoat before leaving, yet she refused, saying she had little time. But rather than the time, the feeling that Anshik was suffering out in the cold had stopped her. If he suffered, she wanted to suffer as well, though it might sound irrational to anyone else.

She checked with his personal assistant to see if he was in the office. The answer was negative. He also told her that he had the office keys. So, there was no way that Anshik would have gone to the office.

The rain thumped her. Her eyes stung with the force of water and mingled with tears of pain. They had lost many years with their misunderstanding.

Driving the vehicle, she checked out if he was at his friends' home, and his circle was small. But he was not with them. She hit the handlebar in frustration as she received a negative reply from them.

Amidst the traffic and rain, she heard her mobile faintly ringing. She stopped her *scooty* at the red signal. There were numerous vehicles in front of her. Recognizing the lengthy stopping time of the signal, she got off her vehicle. The call was from Mrs. Dhawan.

"Hello, aunty."

"Ananya . . ."

"Did you find him?"

"No."

She sounded worried.

"Should we go to the police?"

"What can we tell them, aunty? That a twenty-eight-year-old man is missing for two hours. We know he is angry, but they will not take us seriously, aunty."

"No, Ananya. Mr. Dhawan has some influence on the police department. He will ask them to check."

Just then, a gleaming black helmet from the front caught her eye. She saw a familiar figure removing his helmet to get some fresh air with the long signal. He was soaking wet.

She took a couple of steps in excitement to confirm if it was him. The vehicles honked at her as if she was the one who had blocked the traffic.

"I think it is not required, aunty. I believe I have found him."

"Thank God, Ananya. Sort out your problems and come home soon together. I'll wait for you both."

"Sure, aunty."

She disconnected the call happily. Anshik loved her. She still couldn't believe it. He had denied the fact for a long time, but that was the truth, which made her ecstatic.

She had to convince her father. Anshik was everything to her. She was aware that her father, having repented his earlier actions, was in his listening mode. He arranged her engagement to Rahul because he thought it was the best decision for her. To please her father and overcome her frustration with Anshik, she had given in and nodded earlier. And to her defense, his repeated denial of their love had left her in a state of confusion.

What a blunder she had committed! She had to fix this somehow and get her life going.

Waiting for the signal to turn green, she tried to call him, but he was at the front, and she was far behind. There were too many vehicles blocking her way.

*****

Anshik removed his helmet and placed it at the front. He knew this signal would take some time to get the clearance.

'How dare you, Ananya? To satisfy your father, would you throw me away?

His anger went up a notch. The pouring rain did not cool him, though.

"Sir . . ."

Someone called him. He saw a mother holding a baby, pleading for some money. She hurried to him, tapping the car doors, which did not open for her. The people in the cars did not want to with the pouring rain outside.

"I have to feed him, sir. Please," she begged Anshik.

Though his internal thoughts told him she was capable enough to do physical work, the plight of the baby affected him.

He speculated that the baby was somewhere around eight months old.

"Why are you holding the baby in the rain?" he scolded her.

"Easier for you to say, sir but where will I leave him? I don't have anyone. I need money even for my next meal."

Anshik quickly took out some cash from his wallet so that she wouldn't have to stand in the rain with the baby.

Unknown to him, she pinched the baby from the backside, and it wailed out of pain.

"Sir, look at the plight of the baby. Can you hear its cry? As a mother, I can't. It is unbearable. It appears that God has given you good wealth."

She prompted him, noting his gold chain, ring, and the expensive wet watch.

"Share your good fortune with us. Please help this poor baby."

She pushed the baby close to him, so that its hand stuck to his chain.

Something seemed odd to Anshik. The way she made the baby shiver in the rain and spoke about the baby made him suspect that it might not be her baby at all.

His brain warned him to be on red alert. Retrieving his mobile from the front pouch, he sent his location to a police friend of his.

SOS.

He sent the message.

Moving the baby away from his chain, he inquired, "What are you doing?"

"Who are you?"

"Sir, I don't understand your question."

"Where did you steal this baby?"

"How can you ask this to a mother? It is mine."

"You are wearing a torn sari, and the baby is wearing a torn jumpsuit, but I have noticed the brand. It is costly. How can you afford it?"

"Ha ha. Don't you know, sir? A mother always does her best for the baby."

"He does not even resemble you."

"For God's sake, he resembles his father."

"I don't believe you."

"I don't care. If you are not interested in giving me money, move away. Don't accuse me of false stories," she told him disparagingly.

"No way. You can't go anywhere."

Anshik tried to hold the lady, who stepped back simultaneously. She gestured to the driver in the ambassador behind Anshik's bike.

"He has found out. Do something!" she screamed at him.

The signal turned green.

Before Anshik could suspect the danger behind him, the old car sped up and smashed into him. Thrown out of the bike, he fell to the other side of the road, into the green bushes. He lost consciousness, and everything went black.

"Anshik!" screamed Ananya. She was heartbroken to see the disaster happening right before her eyes but was powerless to stop. Chaos prevailed as the vehicle honked, not realizing that there had been a murder attempt right in front of them.

The traffic police stopped the car, and with the SOS alert, the police joined them.

Dropping her vehicle, she ran to Anshik.

CHAPTER 20

The Beginning

The end is never the end. Flush the past. Live again, creating a new beginning and persevere until you can thrive in life.

With a pounding heart, Ananya rushed to check if he was alright. It took her almost five minutes to reach the spot. The signal was back to red, and the traffic was blocked again. The siren from a police van and the ambulance screamed danger, and the other people stayed back.

With the smart thinking of Anshik, the police had come in at the right time and had rounded up and nabbed the child traffickers.

Meanwhile, Anshik was put on the stretcher and was about to be rolled into the ambulance.

Seeing that they were about to take him away, she panicked and stopped them.

"I will join you," she wailed.

"Who are you? We have already informed his mother."

The police officers stopped her.

"I am his girlfriend."

She cried, looking at Anshik's bleeding face.

"Oh God!" Her concern was genuine, and her face was pale.

"Please . . . we don't have time," she prompted them urgently.

Looking at her pathetic plight, a police officer told her.

"Okay, climb in. But just to ensure that you are not from their gang, I'll come with you."

She was relieved. She did not care what they thought of her.

"Go ahead. We will take care of the situation here," the other police officer told the one in the ambulance.

"Are you sure?"

"Yes, we have caught these two, but it seems they are a part of a big gang. With proper investigation, we could get leads from them to catch the bigger dirty fishes. Sick of these heartless people who use babies as their tools to achieve their mission," he criticized sternly.

*****

Inside the ambulance, Ananya touched him gingerly. His shirt was stained red. Torn partly near his arms, glass pieces were stuck in his chest. The cut seemed deep, and blood trickled from the bruises on his face and glass cuts on his chest.

"No!" she screamed, adding, "Drive faster."

"Relax," the police officer tried to calm her.

"How can I when he is in this state?" she wailed.

Anshik's body shuddered.

"Hold on, Ansh. Don't give up on us."

His body became strangely still, and that doubled her worry.

Ignoring the other people in the ambulance, she threatened, "Don't you dare leave me, Ansh. I cherish you deeply. You are the person behind my success, and I want you till my end. I can't imagine living without you. I love you, Ansh. Please wake up . . ."

What began as a threat ended up as a plea. She held his hands along the way, murmuring words of reassurance and love.

"Don't leave me."

"I love you."

Tears poured from her cheeks. She kept repeating her statements in shock. Her painful rambling brought out tears even from the police officer who had accompanied her.

"Are you Ananya?" he asked.

She nodded, surprised.

"I know. Anshik is my friend. He sent me the location when he suspected that woman. He has spoken a lot about you earlier. We are childhood friends. Don't worry. He loves you."

"Ask him to prove that by coming back to me."

"He will."

His body shuddered again.

Once they reached the hospital, he was taken inside urgently. The Dhawans joined her soon.

The moment she saw Sheela, she ran to her and hugged her with all her might.

His father stood there emotionally. He knew the pain of

being in the hospital, which was not new to him. He patted both their shoulders, lending his support. They waited for an hour.

After a brief inspection and a CT scan, the doctor emerged and informed, "His head has no significant injuries, but his chest is deeply injured. To remove the glass pieces inside, a surgery is necessary. We are still not sure of the extent of the damage."

Mrs. Dhawan whimpered, and Ananya put her hands around her shoulders supportively.

"Don't worry. Dr. Nakul Gupta is a specialist. He will come here soon, and we will operate together to remove them. He's exceptional at his work. But prior to the surgery, we have to perform some more scans."

"Will he be alright, doctor?" Mrs. Dhawan asked anxiously.

"This surgery has a higher success rate if there are no major damages to the internal organs."

"But can't you tell for sure?" Ananya was horrified.

"Let us wait for further results," the doctor concluded.

It was night time. The day had turned absolutely terrible.

"Aunty, don't give up hope. He needs all our prayers and positivity," she whispered.

After all the formal processes, Dr. Nakul Gupta joined the team to perform Anshik's surgery. The waiting hours daunted them. Ananya neither had food, nor did she sleep.

She prayed to Mahadev. *'Please let Anshik live . . . hope the impact of the broken glass is minimal.'*

'Positive affirmation works, Ananya,' she self-instructed.

'Don't give in to negativity.'

She closed her eyes and imagined that the doctor was walking toward her, smiling. She brought in the same vision before her eyes repeatedly.

'Anshik is alright. The surgery is a success.'

She repeatedly chanted the statement as if it was a mantra inside her head. The doctor walked to them. She looked at him, dreading the verdict.

Her positive affirmation had materialized.

"The surgery is a success." He repeated her exact words.

With tears of joy, Ananya hugged Mrs. Dhawan. The burden of weight was lifted away from Mr. Dhawan's shoulders.

"Anshik is alright," the doctor reiterated.

"Can we see him?" they asked.

"No. He is still unconscious and needs rest. We are keeping him under observation to be on the safer side. He might wake up tomorrow."

A little disappointed, Ananya told him, "Alright, doctor."

Once the doctor had left, Mrs. Dhawan turned to her, "Ananya, go home now. You have not eaten. You must be tired."

"No, aunty. I want to be here when he wakes up, and you have not eaten too."

Ankush Dhawan pitched in. "Don't worry, Ananya. I'll get her something from the hospital canteen to eat."

"And, Ananya . . . tomorrow is eighth. Your OTT series is getting launched tomorrow, right?" Sheela Dhawan asked.

She nodded as she recollected it hazily. She had almost forgotten. Their housekeeper came with a pack of rotis and vegetable gravy.

"Mrs. Dhawan, luck is on your side. You have escaped the hospital food," Ankush told her laughingly, relieved that Anshik was alright.

Ignoring his comments on the hospital food, Mrs. Dhawan prompted Ananya, "You need to go, dear. It extends your

227

dream and would be a platform to celebrate the future. As the doctor said, Anshik is out of the danger zone. He should be up anytime. And Kavya will join us soon. She started the moment she heard we admitted Anshik to the hospital. And most of all, Anshik would not like it if he heard you missed the launch because of him."

"Your son does not like a lot of things. One of them is this . . ."

She removed her engagement ring which Rahul had given her.

"Keep this safe, aunty. I have to send it back to my father."

Mrs. Dhawan smiled brightly. "Anshik would be happy when he gets to know."

*****

Ananya could not sleep the rest of the night. She tossed and turned, but sleep eluded her. She was glad he was okay, but her heart cried that he would miss the event. And it was a special day for her tomorrow. She called the producer and let him know that their planned chief guest was hospitalized and could not preside over the function. He had to look for an alternative.

She had fought against society and her orthodox parents to reach this step, and the person who had stood behind her was at the hospital. She sighed.

When her alarm went off, she had barely slept an hour. She had stayed at Anshik's residence ever since her accident.

She dressed up in her sleeveless yellow sheen dress, which reached her knees. Tying her hair into a topknot, she rushed to the door.

"Ma'am," the housekeeper called.

"Toast is ready. Please have some breakfast," she invited.

"*Arre*, Mala. I don't have time. The event begins at nine sharp and I need to check on Anshik."

"Alright, ma'am. But you have an hour still. Please come to the dining room. Let me serve you some toast."

With a brisk nod, Ananya did as Mala asked. With toast on her plate, she called Mrs. Dhawan.

"Hello, aunty, did Anshik wake up?"

"No, not yet, dear."

"Oh, I thought if he was awake, I'd meet him once before attending the event."

"Sorry, Ananya. I am not sure about it."

"Is he alright?" she asked, scared.

"We don't know, Ananya. The doctors have confirmed that the surgery was a success, but they can't tell for sure until he wakes up."

"But yesterday, they told us he was alright," she argued vehemently.

"Yes, they did. But Anshik is not awake still. That has instilled certain doubts in their mind. We are all waiting for him to regain his senses."

"I will come there, aunty. I can't go now," she told her.

"NO."

Her voice was stern. "If he regains consciousness and sees that you have missed your event because of him, it might affect his health negatively and disturb his recovery, which both of us don't want. I know how my son will react if you miss this event. He cares for you, dear."

"I care for him too."

"Show it. Today is your day. Don't miss it for his sake."

With sadness gripping her heart after hearing the news, she took an auto to the Starz Hotel.

*****

The event began with josh, and Ananya took her place grimly on one of the round tables, kept close to the stage. Wearing glittery dresses, her team was having fun.

There was a huge projector on the stage.

The event organizer took control from then on. In her gorgeous pink frilly gown, she kept everyone captivated with small anecdotes that had happened during the shoot. But nothing penetrated her mind, except Anshik's images at the hospital.

Bollywood famous directors and producers graced the occasion, but Ananya did not care. Her thoughts were preoccupied with him. He was there during all her downs, and she wanted him with her today when she stepped up to the next phase in her dream career.

Everyone attending the event promoted the series extensively, and it got the media exposure it deserved.

The event was turning out to be a success, but that did not matter to her. All she craved was the well-being and presence of her man, Anshik Dhawan. With each passing second, she could not control herself. She had agreed to come because of Sheela's insistence, but she could no longer bear it. "And now it is time for the felicitation. We would like to honor the person who was the backbone of this series. She brought it to life. The one who came with this beautiful story and the script and directed it to perfection—Miss Ananya Mehta."

She was supposed to get this award from Anshik. Now a Bollywood biggie stood in his place. She peered at the entrance again, hoping and wishing that Anshik might walk in anytime despite his injuries. But this was not a movie where miracles happen just like that.

Her eyes welled up with tears of disappointment. Her brain processed the fact that he really was not coming. How could she attend this event without him? She did not want to.

Murmuring polite words in the ears of her producer, she left the place as the audience stood stunned by her gesture.

*****

She could not go back to the hospital yet. Sheela would question her about the event. And she might be right. She did not want to disturb Anshik's mental health in case he regained his consciousness.

She checked for new messages on her mobile. There was none from Mrs. Dhawan. She had told her she would message her immediately if he woke up.

Is his health deteriorating then?'

"No, don't go there."

An old man stopped her.

She looked at him questioningly.

"Someone has spotted a crocodile here early morning. Though it is not sure, the officials have issued a warning letter cautioning the nearby fishermen and people."

In her desperation, she had not realized that she had walked toward the Nanded-Shivane bridge, over the Mutha river.

She ignored him and walked further, her thoughts on Anshik.

The elderly man witnessed her madness but lacked the stamina to halt it.

The short bridge was partially submerged underwater because of the significant increase in water levels caused by the rain. It was sloppy all over.

Ananya sat on the rock and cried her heart out.

"Please get well soon, Anshik," she prayed.

'I thought you would walk into the launch event, surprise me, and hand over my shield. But you did not, did you? You have cheated me!' her heart criticized him.

She paused for a second.

'You might have other events, but what if he never wakes up? What if he leaves you? He will not. What if? No . . .'

She tried to calm her chaotic mind, which pelted her with negative thoughts.

Restless, she threw a stone into the river. The water came around in ripples. She heard a weird sound. Then she saw it— the rear part of the torso—tail and back submersed inside. The old man's warning rushed to her mind. Fear took her over, and she froze.

Someone dragged her from behind, and she screamed.

"You are alright. That is not a crocodile . . ."

A familiar voice told her. "They are just a few rocks tinted with the shade of the bushes."

She turned to see Anshik in his hospital dress, with a bandaged forehead and chest, and plasters on his arm. A gush of joy rushed through her as she hugged him hard. Tears of delight flowed down her face as she held onto him.

"If you were scared, why did you come here? The old man told me he had already warned you, but you did not listen."

"It did not matter to me. I was thinking about you."

"Oh God, you are really here!" she exclaimed delightfully.

Ananya pinched herself. "This is not a dream."

"Definitely not a dream. It is not safe to be here, though. Let us not take the risk."

He held Ananya's arms and took her to the spot where he had parked his car on the side of the road, under the tree.

Pink flowers had fallen on the road. The sun slowly peeped out from the clouds as the sunlight touched them warmly.

He swayed a little, and Ananya gripped him tight.

"I think we should go to the hospital first," she ordered.

"We should, but I have something important to do prior to that," Anshik replied.

"Are you alright, Ansh? What is more important than your health? How did they let you leave the hospital?"

He nodded happily. "They did not. I sneaked out."

"Oh God, how dare you risk your recovery?"

"I promise that I will not. Don't worry about me. Let us go back for sure."

She turned her head, stopping him.

"Please, Ananya," he cajoled.

"How did you know I was here?" she asked him, not wanting to hurt him further.

He showed her the watch she wore.

"They are not yours but ma's. I had her smart watch configured, and it helped. I could get your location when I realized you left your event midway."

"Oh, I did not know."

"What were you thinking when you wore it?"

She did not want to hide her feelings anymore. "You. Who else?"

"I know."

"You came to me!" she exclaimed, still unable to believe that he was here for real.

"Where will I go?" He laughed and took out something from his car.

It was her shield that he had collected from the event's manager.

Going down on his knee with a little difficulty, he presented it to her with style under the tree as a gentle breeze wrapped them around. She accepted it with a huge smile on her lips.

"My dear Ananya, we started with nothing years ago. And here we are . . .you've achieved your dream of becoming a director, and I've become a successful entrepreneur. We stood for one another during our testing times, and I want that support till the end. I love you, Ananya— and I promise that I'll take care of you forever and always. Without you, neither this world nor my success means anything, Ananya and you know that deep within. Will you marry me and make me the happiest person in this world?"

Along with the shield, he presented the ring that he had planned to give her back for a long time.

His sincere words made an impact and brought happy tears to her eyes. Her heart was filled with music and joy. With each step, she moved closer and gazed into his eyes.

"I love you too."

"I want to kiss you."

"Not here." She stepped back.

Laughing, Anshik held her tight despite his injuries and kissed her forehead beautifully, stamping her as his forever.

Nature blessed them with a shower of flowers over them.

She tugged his shirt closer and pulled him hard against her.

"The road is deserted. No one is here."

"Are you su—"

His words were lost against her mouth as she pressed her lips against his harder. She was conscious not to disturb his upper body. Their bodies touched gently, and the moment appeared sacred to them. Ananya was sure her heart would swell and blow up if they continued kissing.

His eyes were on fire, and he felt as if their souls had merged at that moment. They wanted to stay in each other's hold forever.

"We need to get you back to the hospital," she reminded him.

Reluctantly, Anshik broke off and said, "Come, let us go. We have another pending task to complete."

Ananya stared at him. "Please don't take any risk, Anshik. I won't be able to bear it if something happens to you."

Her concern touched him. "Give me five minutes and we can go back," he promised.

They stopped at the Broken Trishul temple before getting back to the hospital. Standing before God, they thought about their shared past with fondness.

She looked at him questioningly.

"We have come here to offer our gratitude."

He took a perfectly carved gold Trishul from his car and passed it to her.

"Earlier, we did not have the money to do this, though we longed to. But now we can . . ."

She nodded with glee. Completely satisfied, she went in and removed the Broken Trishul from the idol and replaced it with a golden one.

"Done."

She showed a thumbs-up, and Anshik responded with the same gesture.

Together, they drove back to the hospital.

*****

Six months later . . .

"I am scared," declared Mrs. Ananya Dhawan.

"You should not be, my dear wife," he cajoled.

"Today is the day of Indian television awards."

"And you are the queen of the television. Your TV series is ruling the prime time."

"Not all," she pouted.

"Ha ha, my ever-ambitious wife."

"I am not bothered about it, Ansh. You know about Kishore, right? They have also nominated his TV series along with mine for the best series award."

"Kishore . . . yeah, the guy who stole the script from you. I remember."

"He is cunning and devious, Ansh."

"Does not matter, Anu. Cunningness does not always work. And what is the best he can do? Talent matters. He might have stolen the script from you. Let us see if he could deliver on top of it."

Her heart thudded worriedly. Catching her vibes, Anshik told her, "You should be proud of the way you have stood and delivered. You hold the hearts of many audiences standing along with you."

His words made sense, as usual. "Mr. Anshik Dhawan, I get your point but . . ."

"Don't you remember what I told you?"

"What?"

"I'll kiss you if you ever call me formally."

"But that was ages ago."

"So?"

With that query, he captured her lips in a tender moment. Her worries were forgotten. Not only her worries, but she also forgot almost everything in this world as her hands circled around his shoulders.

Anshik brushed her hair beside her ears and whispered, "I would have kissed you more than a thousand times, yet I don't know why I never feel satisfied and long for more."

"Neither am I, Mr. Anshik Dhawan."

He kissed her again, smiling at her intention.

"My naughty wife . . ."

"Am I?" she pouted.

"Stop tempting me, or I'll not be responsible for my actions."

His lips brushed her forehead tentatively, and he waited for Ananya to deny their pleasure. But she did not.

"If you want me to stop this, tell me now, or we will be late," he murmured in her ears. When she still did not reply, he brushed his mouth against the hollow of her temple at the side.

"Tell me, Anu." He traced her sharp nose with his lips. Her vanilla perfume taunted his self-control.

"Please ask me to stop." His lips were against hers now. She did not do as he requested. Instead, she fell into an imaginary world of ecstasy that sucked her in. Enjoying the heady sensation for a couple of minutes, she pushed him away with regret.

"Let us go," she whispered.

Her husband agreed. "Get ready. We should not be late."

Ananya appeared attractive to everyone in a red sequined gown, with her hair let loose. With Anshik by her side in his ethnic-looking ivory kurta, they made a perfect pair as they walked in calmly and composed. She was not disturbed to see Kishore at the other table. The stage was enormous, and the media coverage was massive. She skipped answering their queries and waited patiently for the award ceremony to begin. Her hands were wet, and the anticipation made her a little nervous.

In her anxiety, she did not note the people who joined her and took their places on the other side of the roundtable.

Anshik held one hand, and someone else had her other hand.

She stammered, "Pa . . . papa."

"Stay calm, *beti*. You will win this for sure."

She touched his feet as he blessed her. Her brother sat along with her father.

"I am sorry, sis," he whispered.

"Both of us must have stood by you. But we did not." The regretful look in her brother's eyes melted her.

Her father went on, "Your mother's letter had a big impact on us, and we noticed how you were struggling to pursue your dreams. Our anger slipped away from us. Anshik brought us here after we called him. Our intention was to surprise you."

"What a pleasant surprise, papa."

"And Anshik is better suited for you."

"Better than Rahul?" she asked him teasingly.

"Way better than Rahul. Anshik is a gem, and you are lucky to have him in your life."

"I know, papa."

The voice from the stage halted their conversation.

"And now for the big moment of truth. It is time for the best television series. There were several contenders, and finally, we have shortlisted two—*Gift of Treachery* by Kishore Khanna, *Start Living Again* by Mrs. Ananya Dhawan."

"To do the honors, let me invite the famous director from Bollywood, Mr. Abhay Chand, to announce the winner."

"And the winner is . . ."

Ananya's heart forgot to beat temporarily. Anshik clasped her hands.

"*Start Living Again* by Mrs. Ananya Dhawan, the show that is ruling the audience at eight in the night daily!"

The audience cheered. She noticed a look of disappointment on Kishore's face. Her father and brother cheered. Anshik hugged her with delight. "You deserve this, and I am proud of you," he murmured in her ears.

"*And I am proud of you, Ananya baby.*" It was not Anshik. She could hear her mother clearly.

For a moment, she could feel her mother's presence around her as if she was near them.

"Thank you, ma . . ." her heart whispered.

Her mother cheered for her. "You did it. You will never have regrets in your life anymore."

Lifting her head, she walked proudly to receive her trophy. This was her dream coming true.

THE BEGINNING

About the Author

A university topper, Saranya Umakanthan is a software engineer by profession and a gadget freak. She is the author of the national bestsellers *One Day, Life Will Change* and *Your Time Will Come,* that captured the hearts of many readers. Having explored the genre of inspiring romance, she believes that she has found her forte. She has penned *Start Living Again* in the same genre.

She hails from Virudhunagar, a small town in Tamil Nadu, and is currently based in Bangalore. With her passion for writing, she wishes to leave an imprint on people's hearts, weaving beautiful stories with her words. She desires to spread positivity with her novels. A romantic by nature, Saranya loves gazing at the night sky while enjoying a cup of coffee. Nothing brings her more contentment than seeing a reader enjoy her book. She's also a gadget freak.

The fragrance and texture of paperbacks inspire her, and she hangs out in bookstores frequently. She would love to hear your feedback.

saranya.umakanthan@gmail.com
@saranya_umakanthan
authorsaranyaumakanthan
chayablossom

More Books by the Author

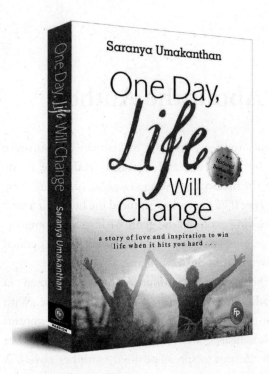

After losing everything she holds dear . . . her love, her parents, and even her singing, Samaira is dejected. She is at her lowest point in life and has no idea what she wants. Vivian is the successful and dynamic head of Creative Tanks and dreams of being the top entrepreneur in India.When their paths cross, sparks fly and they are drawn to each other. The aura of mystery around her tugs at Vivian's heartstrings. While Samaira seems intent on running away from love, hope, and her aspirations, Vivian makes it his mission to bring her back on track. Thus begins an intriguing journey for both, from the end to new beginnings. They chase broken dreams against all odds, inspiring one another. As they walk the arduous path of life, will they climb the ladder of success together? Or will they crash and burn?

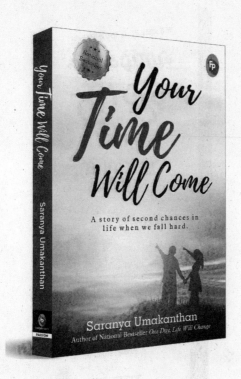

Your Time Will Come

Saranya Umakanthan

National Bestseller

A story of second chances in life when we fall hard.

Saranya Umakanthan

Author of National Bestseller *One Day, Life Will Change*

Love can break the strongest of men and they are the ones to fall hard. But after the fall, will they be able to bounce back and start afresh? Will they ever realize that true love is supposed to "build" them and not "break" them? Siddharth Saxena, a young and dynamic CEO, falls apart when the girl he believes was his, leaves. Depression drives Sid into a web of darkness. His life slips, his business falters, and the world around him shatters. Shanaya enters his life as his wife, unaware of his personal battles. He likes her but does not want to acknowledge the feelings she evokes in him, as he is wary of falling into the trap of love again. But she trusts him and believes that his time will come. He cannot help but be inspired by her positivity which awakens a determination within him. With her by his side, can he rediscover himself and get his life back? Or will he stay broken forever?

Translations

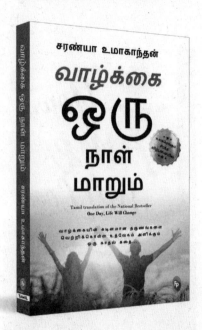